T0278913

ALL THE Love UNDER THE Vast Sky

ALL THE *love* UNDER THE *Vast Sky*

EDITED BY KIP WILSON

Nancy Paulsen Books

Nancy Paulsen Books
An imprint of Penguin Random House LLC
1745 Broadway, New York, New York 10019

First published in the United States of America by Nancy Paulsen Books,
an imprint of Penguin Random House LLC, 2025

Visit us online at PenguinRandomHouse.com.

Library of Congress Cataloging-in-Publication Data
Names: Wilson, Kip, editor, author. | Alessandri, Alexandra, author. | Bowles, David (David O.), author. | Crowder, Melanie, author. | Engle, Margarita, author. | Gansworth, Eric, 1965- author. | Gow, Robin, author. | Lockington, Mariama J., author. | Ruby, Laura, author. | Venkatraman, Padma, 1969- author. | Warga, Jasmine, author. | Waters, Charles, 1973- author.
Title: All the love under the vast sky / Kip Wilson.
Description: New York: Nancy Paulsen Books, 2025. | Audience term: Teenagers | Summary: "Spanning twelve short stories in verse, this collection explores love's many facets and how it manifests in and shapes our lives"—Provided by publisher.
Identifiers: LCCN 2024038768 | ISBN 9780593625279 (hardcover) | ISBN 9780593625286 (ebook)
Subjects: CYAC: Love—Fiction. | LCGFT: Short stories.
Classification: LCC PZ5 .A4564 2025 | DDC [Fic]—dc23
LC record available at https://lccn.loc.gov/2024038768

Manufactured in the United States of America

ISBN 9780593625279
10 9 8 7 6 5 4 3 2 1

BVG

Edited by Stacey Barney and Jenny Ly
Design by Cindy De la Cruz
Text set in Lucida Fax, FS Sammy, Sunday Morning, Neutraface 2 Text, Estilo Pro

To all those waiting for love to arrive:
we present to you the vast sky
—K.W.

Contents

Introduction

By Kip Wilson

Dear Reader,

I'm so pleased to share with you this anthology of stories in verse.

The spark for this collection came from my own personal reading stack. Like many teens, I love quick, digestible reads, especially short stories and poetry, so I've eaten up the great variety of YA anthologies in recent years—seriously, so many good ones! It's the raw emotion of verse novels that makes them my favorite sort of YA book to read. So I thought, wouldn't it be great to combine these two and create a collection of short stories in verse with some of my favorite YA poets.

Of course, the verse format wasn't enough to tie the stories together—we needed a theme. I chose love because, in my poetic heart, nothing is more synonymous with love than poetry. But I also know that love doesn't necessarily mean romantic love, especially to teens, who experience and treasure all kinds of love. We all care deeply about the people in our lives—our friends, our families, and hopefully ourselves. So I asked the authors to keep this in mind and write a story in verse that would fall somewhere under the wide umbrella of what it means to love.

The result is a collection that includes all kinds of love in a variety of settings from India to Mesoamerica to Miami. You'll time travel to past centuries, and you'll encounter teens today embracing loving relationships and found families or feeling the pain of heartbreak and loss. You'll meet mermaids and circus performers, seamstresses and warriors. Best of all, you'll experience some of the varieties of love that have been flavoring the world for hundreds of years—and in the process, you might just discover a new poet or two who speak to you like no other.

Thank you in advance for giving our anthology a chance!

With love,
Kip

Love-Bomb

(v) to lavish someone with attention, especially
in order to influence or manipulate them

By Mariama J. Lockington

When Mom wakes me bright and early
  on my seventeenth birthday
I try to forget that
  I hate her

Hate her as in
  love her so much
looking directly at her
makes my eyeballs ache.

  Her cobalt-Black face radiant
so full of bursting, of too-fast, too-much
  everything now now now
me look at me *me* light

when she smiles

like now:
she is pinching each of my toes
she is saying: *See these perfect toes?*
They are mine I made them
And that sleepy look on your face?

I made that too.

Happy birthday, my sweet Jadine.
Today is the day
I made you you!
Let's make it count.

When I peer at her
from the folds of my covers
all I can make out
is the brilliant aura
surrounding her body.

She's always on some teetering planet
far away from me
sucking up all matter of shimmer
reinventing herself in the morning sun.

I yawn.
It's Saturday, Mom.
It was a late night.
I need sleep.

Mom laughs her I-can't-hear-you laugh.
I made you blueberry-lemon pancakes.
You love those.

I love chocolate chip pancakes.

Blueberry and lemon is *her* favorite.
But I keep this to myself.
I sit up and nod,
taking my braids down from my silk scarf
letting my scalp breathe.
I stretch my long torso, arms high above my head
and Mom sighs in wonder.

Look how graceful you are!
Elegant and beautiful, just like I was as a young girl.
Only I didn't have those things,

Mom says, motioning at my full chest.
I don't know where you got those bazookas from.

Ew, Mom. Stop.
I get my curves from Dad's si—

I bite down on my tongue hard.

Mom's eyes are a tempest.

We don't talk about Dad ever.

So why did I say it?
Maybe a small payback?

We don't talk about Dad ever
the chaos of their toxic relationship
the night he left us when I was ten
or that I have a whole gang of grandparents
cousins, aunts, and uncles
who I never see.

Because
Who needs them!
Mom always yells.
We've got each other. That's what matters.

Sorry. I didn't mean to bring him up,
I mumble
even though she should be the one
apologizing to me for last night
for the mess I'm waking up to
and all the times she's done just this—

greeted me with a fresh smile
a new day
no glimmer of recognition
for how much of my childhood
my adolescence

has been about keeping her safe
for how much loving her
stings.

Sorry is a white flag waving.
A survival song.
A way to keep the delicate peace.

Sorry is a word I'm drowning in.

Never mind that,
Mom starts again, her eyes clearing.
You are the most beautiful daughter
and you are mine.
Let's celebrate!

I nod and
get out of bed
ignoring the trash bag on my floor
full of debris.

When Mom turns her attention on me
like this
when she morphs into super-happy mom
it's impossible to disagree with her
to not match her energy.

Her eyes on me
full of lovely dreams
and a warped truth
I so badly want to be real.

It's hard to grow up with a mother
who is somehow
just a girl

same as me
 but also an adult
 with money to spend
 a car to drive
 scissors and knives

 a brain full of faulty
 chemistry.

But I don't want to fight today.
I want to have a normal birthday.

The kitchen table is a work of art.
 Mom's eye for design,
 a gift. Her penchant for collecting
 pretty things—an obsession.

She's taken out her good china
 her collection of vintage plates and glasses.
 The spotless, dainty silverware.
 The teacups with carefully painted golden leaves
 a matching teapot, not to mention
 the crisp white linen tablecloth
 hand-embroidered with violets and roses.

And in the middle of it all
 a bouquet of sunflowers
their heavy heads drooping deliciously
 toward the sun coming in from the window.

Isn't it the most beautiful table
 you've ever seen?
 Mom claps with delight.

Yes, Mom. The most beautiful.
Thank you.

Sit, sit!
she insists,
snapping into action.
Let me make you a plate.

I raise my eyebrows
at the sunflowers
the only witnesses to this
moment of unfettered attention.

Never mind that most mornings,
I'm the one up first.
The one making eggs for her.
The one bringing her coffee,
making sure she gets to work on time.

Eat up,
Mom says as she places an enormous stack of pancakes
in front of me.
Then she drizzles them with too much syrup
and kisses me lightly on the head.
After this, I'm taking you shopping.

Mom—thanks, but this is a lot of pancakes.
You don't want any?

Oh, no. Not on my diet.
You go ahead.

Mom sits, her plate empty,
and watches me take each bite.

The pancakes are sticky on the roof
of my mouth, the syrup
        too sweet
the acid from the berries and lemon
already making my stomach twist.

When it's dark
our house becomes enemy territory.
Mom draws invisible lines
        explosives hidden everywhere in the shadows.

I never know where to step
        or what to say
or how my breathing   too loud
or too soft   might set Mom off.

That's why I fled last night
my girlfriend, Marie, waiting down the street
        car lights off, music low.

I'd tried to be honest for once.
To say: *Marie is taking me out.*
To celebrate. A party.
I'll be back by one a.m.

But Mom had just snarled
You really think
        Marie cares about you?
Nobody loves you like I do, Jadine.
        Just remember that.

I'd come out to Mom
in seventh grade

and all she had said was
Date who you want.
I don't care!

But then I stumbled into Marie
    one day freshman year
as we both hurried through the massive hallways
    of our high school, late for fifth period.

Marie was new—
    I was a recluse
but somehow when she smiled at me
    I felt like we'd known each other
    before   like maybe in another life
    she'd been a drop of dew
    and I a parched peony
    both of us glistening
    and soaking into each other
    under an intense sunrise.

Soon,
    we were inseparable.
Wherever Marie was
    I was.
We became an item—
    all my secrets
    all her scars
    all our dreams
    and nightmares
    laid out before each other
    without judgment.

Then Mom
    found us one afternoon

whispering love-words
to each other in my room
    kissing in between
solving equations for math class.

I don't want that girl
    anywhere near my house, you hear?

I don't care that you're gay.
    But not her.
    She's not good for you.
    She's poisoning your mind against me.
    I can feel it. In my bones.
    You're different around her.
        She's changing you.

That was the first time I
    slammed my door in Mom's face.
I'm different because I'm growing up!
    I yelled through the barricade.
I know what I want. Who I am becoming.
    You can't stop me from living!

But Mom just laughed,
    cackled really.
You're pathetic. A pathetic slut.
    You don't know anything about life.

Maybe she's right,
    but I do know this:
    Marie doesn't try to buy my affection
    or withhold hers
    when I don't do or say
    exactly as she does.

She asks me questions
listens to my answers.
She remembers small things
like how I hate all berries
but will tear up a box of
Little Debbie cakes in minutes.

She's the only one who knows
my deepest desire
how I want to live
by the Pacific Ocean one day
see those trees that are so tall and big
you can drive right through them.

She's the only one who knows
how lonely it feels to keep this dream quiet
to always be dulling my shine
for a mother
I know I can't leave behind.

And Marie never tells me what to do.
She only says *I hear you. I love you.*
There's so much world out there to see.
You deserve to feel connected to it all.

So, when I slipped into Marie's car
to head to the party despite Mom's protests
all the malice of her words
dissipated.

You know you don't belong to anyone
but yourself?
Marie said, grabbing my shaking hand
after I buckled in.

This is your life. Your night.
Not hers.

Then Marie hit the gas
and the farther we got from home
the easier my breath came.

At the party,
I danced hard.
Hurling my body like a comet
through the dark crowd.
Marie at my side doing the same.

The two of us hardly touching
but still so close
our whirling and stomping
and dipping a kind of prayer
a celebration of skin and hips and teeth
and all the things we cannot change
thrown off our necks like sweat.

When midnight rolled around
I was joy-wasted.
Marie dragged me to a quiet corner
of the backyard and produced
a Zebra Cake from her bag,
a candle, and a lighter.

Make a wish,
she said, lighting the flame.

I squeezed my eyes shut
took a deep breath
then blew the light out.

In the dark of my wish
I kissed Marie until our lips
were too raw to continue.

Happy birthday, she whispered
into my neck.

And for a moment,
it really was.

Then Marie said,
Next year when we graduate
come with me.
We can go out of state
together.

I pressed my forehead hard against hers
allowing myself
for just a moment
to imagine myself free to go
our lives together   full of
unsupervised dorm room hangs
nights out   art museums
and other adventures.

It's just the two of us, I barely whispered.
You know I can't. She needs me.

Marie was quiet   but I could feel
the aching in her gentle gaze
as she lifted my chin
and brought our lips together
for a soft kiss.

Okay, she said after, as she took my hand.

Well then,
let's not waste the time we do have.

So we returned inside to the party
and danced ourselves back to euphoria.

Mom was up when I got home
from the party.
Every light in our little bungalow on,
an eerie before-battle silence filling the air
as I shut the door behind me.

From the back bedroom hallway
I heard a shuffle and slam.
I made my way toward it like a mouse.

Mom?

No response.
Then the TV in her room clicked on.
Her door shut tight.

I'm home.
Good night, I love you,
I said through the closed door.

Mom turned up the volume.

I used our shared bathroom,
brushed my teeth, washed my face
and then tiptoed into my room, across from hers.

When I flipped on the light,
I saw what she had left me:

every one of my graphic tees
yanked from my dresser
        cut into hundreds of
                jagged pieces
        littered all over my floor.

I was too tired to cry.
Instead, I got a trash bag,
stuffed all the remnants inside.

Then I rolled into my covers
and let the darkness hug me close.

I thought maybe
        we could get you some new clothes?
Mom smiles, rushing toward H&M.

We are at the mall downtown.
My stomach bloated with birthday pancakes
my head throbbing from a sugar crash.

Mom is already riffling through a rack.
How about this one? she says,
holding up a tee with Diana Ross on the front.

Before I can say yes, she tosses it
        over her arm into a cart
and is on to the next.

This one's cute too.
I see all four of the Beatles' faces
        crumpled into her arms.

I don't even like the Beatles,
I mumble under my breath.

This one is cute! It has a Black Barbie on it,
she continues.

Mom, no, you know Barbie is not my vibe.

Oh, hush. You'll look so cute in this.
If I say you'll love it, you'll love it.

But—Mom, it's my—

But Mom is running to another rack.

I don't follow.
I stand, grazing my hands
over a display with sunglasses
and earrings.

I don't belong to my body.
I watch   as Mom adds
more and more clothes to the cart
all the while talking out loud
to herself
or maybe she means to be
talking to me?

Either way, other customers are staring.
It is too hot in my skin   I'm dizzy.
I want to yell:
MIND YOUR BUSINESS.

I want to yell:
Can't you see? This is her way of saying:

I'm sorry.
I love you so much it wrecks me.
I hurt you because I can't reckon
with my own wounds.

But I don't say anything. Instead I take one more look
at my mom, burying herself
under a mountain of clothes.
I take one more look at a woman
fraying at her edges
and me, a child, following her
trying to collect all the
runaway threads   scraps of love I can.

I take one more aching look   hoping that maybe
she'll pause   turn and realize
I'm not happy.

See me see me see me see me see me,
my heart pounds.
But she doesn't.   She never does

so I walk

away
out of the store
and out of the wing
of the mall entrance we parked at
and I keep walking
until I'm at the empty bus stop
off the main road.

I sit, startled to find
my face is wet with salty tears.

I sit and let them fall
like a gift   I didn't know I needed.
I think about Marie's large hoops
    tickling my shoulders when
    she leans in to kiss me.
    Her locs fragrant with argan oil
    her embrace a balm
    about her holding my hand, saying:
    You belong to yourself.
    You deserve to see the world.
    This is your life, not hers.

I think about
    coastline winding
    the Pacific dressing herself
    in all shades of orange, teal, and gray
    as the sun dips low.

And me
    completely alone
collecting stones bearing my namesake
    on a rocky shore.

My hands full of
    delicious green jade
    sand and wind
    twisted driftwood
        pointing in all directions.

A whole coastline to call mine
    the blue never ending.
Freedom in every step I take
    toward myself.

    When the bus comes, I am ready.

I wipe my face and step on.
I settle into a seat in the back,
and as the bus pulls away from the curb
toward home
I take out my phone, open Google, and type:

Top 10 Colleges in the Pacific Northwest.

I'm sorry, Mom,
I whisper.

But one more year
and I'm gone.
I'm not drowning for you.

And the words fly out of my mouth
and into the gray sky
like a murder of crows.

All for Annie

BY ROBIN GOW

United States, late 1800s

Wagon Trek

We've just begun our circus's third
tour across America,
complete with new wagons
for performers
and a new, even huger big top.

The earth is damp and muddy
from thunderous summer rain that fell last night.

I always wake up before everyone else
to cook breakfast for the troupe.

My brilliant
wonderful
daring
little circus family.

Those early days starting the show were tough
but now we have enough money to buy
all kinds of ingredients for me to create meals from—
it makes the task exciting
each and every morning.

I only take a moment
to brush my long hair
and glance at myself

in the small hand mirror Ella gave me
last Christmas.

My skin is soft—cheeks round.

I run a hand through my beard.
Take a dab of perfume,
then a dab of oil
to keep the hair from becoming coarse.

I wonder what I might look like
without it—like
other eighteen-year-old girls?

I guess I might
but I am the bearded lady, after all.

I wouldn't be here without my beard—
funny how some hair can change
a person's life. Open all kinds of doors for her.

Still, I guess it's just human nature.
I can't help but wonder
who I'd be without it.

I set my fire far away from the tent.
I always do
so I don't risk a strong wind
catching some cloth
and sending the whole place up in flames.

Add pork cut in hearty chunks to the pan,
then eggs fried in the sweet grease.

I start the batter for pancakes,
my very favorite part.

I stop.

Something feels amiss.

Silence all around.

Maybe just the disappointment
of not doing a show last night.

No one ever comes out to see us
if there's a storm.
Instead, we read books
and tell stories in the dark.

I look up from the sizzling first pancake
and see Felipe, one of our horse riders,
running from the sleeping tent.

He's weeping and shouting,
"Annie! Annie!
I need your help!
It's Ringmaster Murphy!
He's not waking up!"

Silence in Murphy's Trailer

I stand over his body.
It's just me and Felipe
in Murphy's trailer.

The trailer has one window
and morning light
spills across the floor.

I know that Felipe
often wakes Murphy up
if he's sleeping too late.

Murphy likes to get up early
to survey the ground
and get ready for whatever tasks
we have to complete.

He's always one of the first
to check on breakfast too.

Murphy isn't in bed.

He's on the floor.

Shattered glass
is scattered everywhere.

I check his pulse.
"He's dead," I tell Felipe.

"No, he can't be," Felipe argues.
"He just has to wake up!"

I hold Felipe
as he cries.

I wish I could cry too
but I hold it in.

I want to comfort Felipe.

He's only two years
younger than me
but I feel protective of him.

I keep thinking,
How could this happen?

Murphy was old but not
that old. He was only forty.

We have no plans
for what would happen
if he were gone
because we couldn't imagine
something like this happening.

Already,
my mind is spinning.

Who will be
our ringmaster?

"I'm going to tell the others,"
I say to Felipe
once his breathing evens out.
"Can you ride into town
and see if you can get ahold
of the coroner?"

Felipe nods solemnly.

"Hey," I say.

He looks up.

"We're going to be okay,"
I say even though I'm not sure
if it's true.

Murphy's Big Top Extravaganza

We've had to work hard to earn our name
as one of the most famous
traveling circuses
in the country.

But we'd be nothing without Murphy.

In our first year,
when we didn't make enough
on a show with a tiny audience,
he used his own money
to buy us bread to share.

But there were so many hungry nights.

I worked hard
to stretch what little food we had.

I bartered my sewing skills
for vegetables at local markets.

Together, we chopped cabbage and potatoes
and peppers and onions.
I instructed the others
on family recipes.
We made thick stew.
Licked our bowls clean.

Still, hungry as we were,
we were joyful,
laughing and singing
by the fire. Our shadows
dancing on the cool night earth.

I am not sure how we'll get on
with no ringmaster.

I don't want to go back
to being hungry every night.

He was always the one who could
keep morale up even when times were rough.

Of course, we have all our talents.

We have the clowns:
Bop, Jimmy, and Beetle.
The gentle animal tamers:
Pineapple and Larry.
The young horse riders: Raul and Felipe.
Our expert gunslinger: Dead Daisy.

Then there are the acrobats.
They're the most recent additions.
Sisters Elise and Ella.

Ella, who is the sweetest
and gentlest of all humans.
Whose amber eyes
dazzle me in the sun.
Ella, who I want to ask,
*Would you like to take a walk with me tonight
now that the show is over?*

Ella, who I can't seem to work up the courage
to speak to much beyond pleasantries
and passing conversations
and compliments like
"You were marvelous tonight."

Yes, we are a spectacular bunch.
Creative and strange.

But Murphy booked our shows.
Mapped our routes
and handled
all the finances.
On top of all that,
he was the ringmaster!

The face of the whole show.

His name was the one people recognized
that started to skyrocket us to notoriety.

I'm going to hold on, though,
and do what I can
to try to keep us together.

I'm terrified
that without Murphy
this little family I've found
will fall
apart.

Farewell, Murphy

I go from tent to tent
to tell everyone in the circus.

They mostly react the same
as Felipe, not willing to believe

a man like Murphy
could be gone in an instant.

Pineapple weeping in my arms.
Larry saying, "We have to call a doctor."

I hold myself together for them.
I say, "We're going to be okay.
We're going to figure this out."

Felipe brings
the coroner to take Murphy's body.
Since we don't have the money
to put on a real funeral,
the coroner will have him buried
in their church's plot.

I know he's gone
but seeing his body
carted away from our circus
feels so permanent.
In the moments after his body departs
we're all still shocked—

still mourning him—
still not quite believing

he's really gone.

Even though I saw the body,
let the coroner carry him away,

a piece of me keeps hoping
he'll walk right through the tent flap

and say,
"I sure scared you, didn't I?"

It's Only the Afternoon

Finally, I return
to my own trailer.
I collapse on my bed
and sob.

I bury my face
in my pillow.

I hear a soft knock on my trailer door.
"Annie, are you there?"
It's Ella!

Quickly, I collect myself.
I don't want to look
like a mess when I see her.

I open the door. Try to look steady.
I've always been Murphy's biggest helper
but it's usually in ways
people don't often notice.

My fellow performers already turn to me
to make sure there's food to eat
and costumes cleaned for the show.
They're going to need even more from me now.

I don't know if they could
ever see me as important like Murphy, though.

Plus, I don't know everything Murphy did.

"We're gathering under the big top,"
Ella says.

Her face shifts.
"Are you all right?" she asks.

I break down. I shake my head.
"No," I admit.

I'm so embarrassed.

I didn't want to show my weakness to her.

"Come here," Ella says.

She embraces me.
"I know you always try
to be strong for us.
Just let yourself cry.
I won't tell anyone."

I do and I'm so grateful
for Ella.

Family Meeting

It's only been hours since
we found Murphy dead
when we gather under the big show tent
to talk about what to do.

Bop the clown says, "Would be easier
without this whole to-do weighing us down.
Coordinating everyone's acts
and traveling with so many people
is a whole production. We clowns could
bop around easier on our own."

My heart sinks.
I love our whole show.

I think it's beautiful
to move like a flock—like a herd.

"No!" I stand up.
I'm embarrassed to make such an outburst
but I don't understand how they
can be talking like this.
It's not like the tent caught fire.
Murphy was our kind and brilliant leader
but it was all of us who made the show.

We'll have to work hard
to gain fame again without him at the helm
but it's not impossible.

I try to stay composed
and ladylike, but this is not a time for that.

Everyone looks at me but no one speaks.
Finally, Ella breaks the silence

with her soft voice. "I don't want to split up . . .
It's not what Murphy would want.
He'd want us to stay together.
Think of all those wonderful nights
singing by the fire. Days when
Murphy would congratulate each of us
on a wonderful performance.
We'll never have a ringmaster
like Murphy, but we don't have to
throw out all those beautiful things
just because he's gone."

Jimmy the clown scoffs,
"That's because
you wouldn't make it out there
in the world without this show
propping you up. Annie and Ella, you're
young and naive; what are you both,
seventeen? Eighteen? I've been
performing for nearly twenty years."

Beetle adds, "Murphy was always picking up
little performers like you just to be kind."

My heart turns
to a knot of anger.

I'm the one
who cleans the costumes
and makes the food and lights the lamps
and buys the soap.
They have to know
I've been Murphy's right-hand person.
Do they not see that?
Is it because I'm young? A girl?

Dead Daisy says, "Well, we have
a show here next weekend, don't we?
Why don't we try it without Murphy
and see if we can pull it off."

What Could Be Our Last Show

As a crew we agree
to postpone a decision
until next weekend.

We'll put on the show
without Murphy
and see how it goes,

then decide if we really
want to stay together.

Dead Daisy came up with the idea,
always trying to mediate between
the grouchy clowns
and dreamy acrobats
and horse riders and me.

Maybe performing
will remind everyone
of the glory we've shared together.

Those first times
we filled the tent
with paying guests
who cheered our every act.

But for the first time in years
I feel nervous
about a performance.

Monday

Time rushes past.

All week
we barely practice—
everyone too heartbroken
to think of performing.

On Thursday
we finally meet
to figure out how to run our acts
without Murphy announcing everyone
and doing his jokes
and quips in between.

"I guess we can just
introduce ourselves,"
Larry suggests.

"Might take people
out of the experience,"
Dead Daisy says.
"I like to not speak."

I hold up my hand
to get everyone's attention
and see it's shaking.

I don't want to be nervous.
I know this team.
I've done
so much of what Murphy has.
Why am I so worried
to contribute my ideas?

But all I can think is
who is going to want to see a circus
without a ringmaster?

The Beard

When I joined the show,
it was just me, the clowns

and the animal tamers,
and, of course, Murphy.

Murphy said,
"Every circus needs
a good freak show act,"
when he introduced me.

The clowns recoiled and laughed.

I touched my beard—
the soft and spilling cascades of brown hair
more beautiful even than the hair
on most ladies' heads.
I wanted people to see
there is nothing so strange
about a woman having a beard

but at the same time
I needed them to see it as strange
for me to make my livelihood.

I used to not like the word *freak*
to describe rare and wonderful
people like myself
but now I kind of feel
a fondness for it because
it's a word I've reclaimed.

It was a hard time
working every single day
with people gawking
and laughing at me

but at night
I loved to go out and stare

at the wild blue-black sky
and think how far I'd come.

Ella

When I first met Ella
I knew she was going
to drive me mad.

She has short curly hair
and a pixie-like
disposition.

To see her fly through the air
is to glimpse
an angel. I watch her

each performance in awe.
I always want to ask her,
Do you think you could love

another woman? Something about her energy
feels the same as mine. The way her body

unfurls for each day.
Her light. Her curiosity.
What I really want to ask is

Do you think you could love
another woman, with a beard?

Because even if she loves women
could she love a woman
like me?

One morning at breakfast
Ella out and said,
"I appreciate you so much, Annie."

She continued, "You do so much
for our little family and I don't think
anyone ever thanks you."

I thought I was going to fall over right there.
Ella flushed and held my gaze

for a moment
two
three.

I hold out hope
that maybe Ella
could see me differently.

I dream of us sleeping side by side
blanketed by
the dark and deep night.

Ringmaster

Everyone is dressed and ready
when we gather for dinner before the show.

I'm wearing my favorite corset
and wine-purple dress—bows tied
all down my beard.

I've made
corn bread and beef stew,

ears of local corn
broken so that everyone
will get a piece.

I pass the serving bowl around
as we all get settled.

I can tell everyone is nervous.

No one knows who
should speak first.

Will the show really
go all right if we don't have
a ringmaster?
Could any of us do it?

Finally, Jimmy the clown says gruffly,
"I guess I'll do it—
I've been around
since Murphy started this show.
I know the most.
I can handle it. I'll be ringmaster."

There's a long silence.
No one is objecting
and I don't want to be
the only one

but I know Jimmy and the other clowns
aren't right for this. Mostly,
their joking feels like sibling banter
but sometimes it goes too far.

Sure, it makes the audience laugh
but it makes us performers feel

so down afterward
and scared to mess up
the next show. It's not
what a ringmaster should do.

Once, Ella slipped on the way down
from one of her dismounts.
She fell on her face—
dirt and clay all in her mouth—

the clowns came out
teasing her and mimicking
how she'd fallen.

I feel a pang of anger
remembering how Murphy
had let that happen.

Dead Daisy cuts in and says,
"Now hold on.
Let's really think about this."

Jimmy's face flames red.
"Oh, now you want to talk?
The clowns are the only performers here
who've been around long enough
to know how this works."

Dead Daisy, always ready for a gunfight,
puts her hands on her hips.
"Now, Jimmy, we know
that's not true."

"Remember, we're doing you a favor
by sticking around—we still might

just take our show
and start off on our own."

Dead Daisy says,
"You could do us a *real* favor
and leave. All you've done
is put people down."

Jimmy scoffs,
"We'll see how well you do
without Murphy *and* us.
You have no ringmaster
and no comedy. Ha!"

The clowns storm off.

I guess they don't view the circus
the same way the rest of us do,
as a real family.

What About *Me*?

After a moment of silence
as the clowns' absence settles in,
Ella's sweet voice
rises, desperately.
"What about Annie?"

Everyone stops and looks at me.

My face turns red.

"What if Annie were the ringmaster?
Well, more like ring mistress, right?"

Elise chimes in, "Oh, sounds risqué.
I like it."

Everyone is chattering, and light returns to their voices.
Larry says, "Annie helped Murphy
book shows."

Felipe adds, "Annie
helped price tickets
and plan our travel route."

"Come to think of it,
Annie helped Murphy
with everything," Dead Daisy says.

I hear what they're saying
but I'm asking myself, *Could I really do it?*

I don't want to hold us back.

Pineapple says, "Think of how unique we'd be!
Not only the best acts in the country
but also led by a fabulous bearded lady!"

"A truly one-of-a-kind show," Felipe says.

I survey my fellow performers—my family.
Ella gives me a gentle smile and a nod
and I decide I am going to try—
I have to for them.

Maybe I know more than I think I do.

"And after the show
we can count the money together?" Raul asks
with hesitation.

"I wouldn't have it any other way," I say.
"That's only fair."

"Let's hear it, then!" Dead Daisy says.
"All for Annie!"

Ring Mistress

The moment I enter the performance area,
all my doubt falls away like flower petals.
I see the rows of audience members—
eyes glinting with excitement
and wonder. Children
with mouths wide open
as they witness me,
a bearded woman, taking center stage.
I wear the same outfit I usually do
but I use Murphy's cane
to gesture
all around. I raise it
and it feels like I'm a conductor—
conjuring music from our guests
and the performers alike.
I beam as I say, "Welcome! Welcome!
We have quite a show for you tonight
at the Big Top Extravaganza!"
Applause floods the space
and I spread my arms
and puff out my chest
feeling just as big
if not bigger
than Murphy
to introduce the first act.

Counting

After the show, all the performers gather
and we count dollars and coins together,
making little piles in the center of us all.

I thought it would probably be
twenty dollars or so, but as we count, the number climbs.
Raul says, "Thirty!"
finishing his pile, and Pineapple
gazes in awe at his little stacks of quarters.

"To be honest," Raul says, "I've been wondering
why we haven't been making more money
when we've been doing
sold-out shows night after night."
Felipe tries to calm him, saying,
"Let's just take a second—"

"No," Raul says, cutting Felipe off.
"I want answers."
There's a long silence again.

When we finish counting
there's about a hundred dollars in total.

We're all excited but also filled with
sadness and resentment, knowing
Murphy stole so much from us.

"I wonder where all that money went," Dead Daisy says.

Raul sighs. "We'll probably never know."

"His trailer!" I snap my fingers.

We still haven't had the heart
to go through it.
We used the normal cash box tonight
but maybe all that money he skimmed from our earnings
is stashed somewhere.

We dash over there together
and inspect every inch
of Murphy's trailer.

We're about to give up
when I find a red leather suitcase.
I feel its heft.

"I think I found something," I say.

Ella hugs me
from behind as I open
the latch and discover
rows and rows
of bills. More money
than I've ever seen.

Under the Stars

I feel weightless
as I step out into the cool desert night.
Rich purple-black sky.

Now I'm the only one awake.
The others went to sleep
not long after the show.

It was such an achievement.
We performed without the clowns

and the show's success
is wonderful proof
we don't need them.

I hear footsteps
and I leap to my feet—
suddenly aware that
I am a young woman
in the dark alone.
"Who is it?" I ask fearfully.

"Only me," Ella says
with a voice like white lace.

"I thought everyone was asleep,"
I say, my heart doing backflips
in my chest.

"Not me. Unless this is a dream."
She pauses. "It would be
a lovely dream. It's so nice out."
She pauses again.
"And perfect to share
a night like this
with you."

I feel as if I am going to faint.
I ask her, "Do you want
to sit with me?"

"Of course," Ella says.
"I came out here to tell you something."

"Oh?" I ask, trying to sound calm.

"I was so glad to see you
leading the show with
your love. You make me proud
to be a performer."

I dissolve in her kindness,
playing with my beard nervously.
I've never been good at taking compliments
but I manage a "Thank you.
You're stunning, Ella.
So stunning."

"Nothing like you, though," Ella says.

I nudge her shoulder and laugh.
"Bah! You're an acrobat. That takes
so much skill and training. I could never.
I only have this beard."

"It's not just the beard, though—
you put on a show! You're a ringmaster
and a model."

I cackle. "A model. Imagine me
like one of those showgirls."

"That's the kind of showgirl
I want to see," Ella says, and my face flushes.

A long silence swells between us—
I imagine us suspended in midair
like those moments when
she and Elise let go of their bars,
moving to grab each other.

She slips her hand around mine
and asks, "How's this?"

I nod, tears trickling down my face.
"It's good. I always hoped," I say.

"You like this?" Ella asks,
holding up our clasped hands.
"So, what about this?"
She looks into my eyes
before moving in
to kiss me.

I can't believe this is real
and that Ella really feels for me
what I've felt for her all along.

I think of the days of strife
when I thought I would always be alone.
I felt so much joy just knowing Ella
but for so long I've wanted us
to be more than fellow performers

and now, here with her,
I know someone will lift me up for who I am.

When we run out of things to say,
we walk together, let the wild and star-crowned sky
swallow us whole
as we amble between cactuses
and then, finally, find our way back
to the tent to rest.

We Are the Briar

BY LAURA RUBY

December 1917

Winter

—is not my season. Wet, stinging cold,
    needles of sleet savage enough to draw

blood. The train car is an icebox. I gather
    my collar tighter in a gloved hand, pink

index finger peeking from a tear in the worn
    black leather. My breath makes clouds on the

window glass—clouds in the shape of a sheep,
    clouds in the shape of a wolf, clouds in the

shape of a heart. But if you were to ask Stepmother,
    I have no heart to give, or to break.

And, as if to prove her right, the heart on the glass
    vanishes. Stepmother clicks her tongue but

I will not look at her, I will not look at Arabella
    or Lucille, my stepsisters, the three of them

huddled on the seats across from me like a fist
    of white mushrooms on a felled, rotting log.

I keep my eyes on the ghostly blur of trees and hills
    outside. The sleet turns to snow as the train

grinds north, leaving New York City behind, to bring
me to Briarcliff, where I will be left behind.

Bird in the Pot

The letter came a month ago, an estranged
aunt's surprise but urgent invitation

to her estate in Tarrytown, New York,
for one last New Year's celebration. *Bring*

yourselves to Briarcliff. I expect your
company and conversation. For sure,

my stepmother smelled "inheritance," said,
"I think your aunt Louisa's not long for

this world." She told her girls, Arabella
and Lucille, that they must offer aid and

consolation first to secure their share,
ensure their futures. Arabella scoffed,

"Am I a nurse, Mother, or a dotty
old woman's companion? What is it you

believe *we* can do?" They didn't know I
was eavesdropping behind the kitchen door

with Cook, the only ally I had left.
We heard Stepmother's contempt, her smirking

self-congratulations: "You'll be the most
gracious young ladies your aunt has ever

seen. As for the care and consolation
Aunt Louisa needs, we shall bring Bird. She's

no lady: who'd believe she's any relation?
But she'll do as an old woman's maid.

And it will get her out from under our
feet." Cook's soft voice went rough as fire-

baked bricks around the hearth. "If *they* are what
ladies should be, then who would want to be

a lady?" She held my face with hands that have
wrung the necks of geese and ducks and plucked them

clean, roasted and served the tenderest meat,
and boiled the bones for soup. *I* was the bird

in the pot now, stewed and steeped, for the last
slurps of marrow. Cook had let me cry for

what was stolen, what was sold: my mother,
my father, my oak tree, my dogs and my

horses, my mother's red velvet cape and
her filigree necklace, my father's last name.

But I have not cried since. Refuse
to give them the satisfaction.

How to Travel in High Style

Arrive at the Tarrytown station in the thick
    of a blizzard, where you are met by a hearse-

like carriage—creaking, ancient—instead of the spit-
shined black Cadillac your step-people expected.

Sigh as your not-family barks and whines
when the young coachman—impatient—crams their snow-
slick trunks into the cab and hands the
mewling trio inside, no room
for you and no choice but to

climb up beside the gruff, sullen coachman.
Accept the gray woolen blanket—tattered, faded—
he tosses your way before he snaps
the reins, begins the drive.

Bury yourself in the cover's coarse
weave. Your lashes freeze but this white-
out world—sparkling, quiet—smells warm
as horses.

The Eyes of Briarcliff

I gasp when I see it, gathering itself
from the frenzied air. Not a house but a castle
pitched
against the icy moat of the Hudson.

"It's something, innit?"
says the coachman, the first words
he's spoken in more than an hour.

"The candles in the windows
look like eyes," I tell him.

"Aye. I always wonder: Do you see
the Briar or does the Briar see you?"

When the carriage finally stops
at the entrance, I thank the coachman
for the blanket and the scintillating
conversation. He cocks an eyebrow
and asks my name. My real name
is the only thing I have left.
I tell him he can call me Bird,
everyone does.

“Everyone like that noisy lot
we’ve been dragging through the storm?”

As if summoned, Arabella bangs
on the walls of the carriage below.
“Boy! Do you intend to assist us or
are we to break our necks on this wretched ice?”

He shakes his head. Behind the veil
of snow, he might be a few years older than I—
maybe nineteen, maybe twenty. He says,
“How did you end up working
for a useless lot like that?”

“It’s a long and sordid tale, I’m afraid,” I say.

“Maybe”—his lilting voice its own kind
of ride—“one day you’ll want
to tell me.”

When We Stormed the Castle

They saw:

One stepmother, yellow-haired, thin-
lipped, sharp-cheeked.

Two golden stepsisters, both taking in the richness
of the furnishings and the straight backs
of the servants, all three measuring for draperies
in the dark.

One shivering, dark-haired
girl, rumpled as burlap,
straggling in after.

I saw:

A foyer with slick marble floors and
damasked walls, a fixture the size of
a planet tinkling softly overhead but offering
no light. Two maid-servants in starched aprons,
each holding a candle. A woman with iron-
gray curls and pink-pinched
cheeks—her neck draped in a raccoon-fur stole
that won't stop staring—holds up a glass, toasting
herself.

"Welcome! I am Miss Louisa Wright,"
she slurs. "And who, pray tell,
are all of you?"

What You Say, What You Don't

If you're Stepmother, you offer a rare,
indulgent smile—the one she used to woo
your father, the one she's since folded up
and stowed away—and you say:

"I am Mrs. Noah Wright, your sister
by marriage, and these are my daughters,

Arabella and Lucille."

Miss Louisa Wright blinks, totters,
sloshing liquid on the floor.
"Huh," she says. "I thought you'd be
younger." With her glass, she gestures
to me. "And who is that little
frozen thing?"

Arabella says, "Oh, that's Bird, our—"

"Maid," finishes Stepmother. "We took her
in when she lost her parents."

If you're me, you lift your face to the light
hoping that Miss Louisa will see your father
written there. She says, "Did you fish her
out of the Hudson?"

If you're Lucille, you titter. If you're me,
whatever hope you had spirals away
like snow. She doesn't recognize you. Or
doesn't care.

Miss Louisa Wright says, "Maid or not,
she needs to warm up. Follow me
to the parlor."

If you're me, you try not to shiver
too hard, afraid you resemble nothing
so much as a half-drowned stray.
You do not say, *My father took*
them *in*. You do not say, *I am*
nobody's maid.

Cousins of Cousins of Cousins

My feet are so numb I trip into the parlor, and
into the arms of a man tall and fair, with eyes

the color of strong tea. "Here," he says, "let me."
He leads me to a chair by the blazing fire and

sits me down. He kneels in front of me. Finger
by finger, he tugs the gloves from my stiff

hands. "Better?" he says. All I can do is nod;
all Stepmother can do is glare. He stands and

bows. "I'm Paul Darbonne. Cousin of a cousin
of a cousin. You know how that is." I do not

know, but I do not care. He's so handsome
I forget my name. He adds, "I hope I'm seated

next to you at supper." Aunt Louisa says,
"Supper is a fabuful idea. Wonderfab."

She stamps her foot. "Paul! Why are my words
not working?" Mr. Darbonne stands and takes

her empty glass. "Words are slippery things,"
he says. "Perhaps you are tired?" Aunt Louisa's

raccoon looks concerned. So do the servants.
Aunt Louisa answers, "Stop fussing, Paul.

I am fline. Line. *Fine.*"
Stepmother's eyes shine.

Spells

I'm not long for my seat
next to the fire, or for Mr. Darbonne's
unexpected attentions. Stepmother
orders me to the kitchens, to help
the other maids serve dinner.

The electricity has been out
for hours, but the food is hot. I pour wine,
ladle soup, scoop potatoes. My own belly
clenches in hunger, but I'm told I will
not eat till "my betters" are
finished.

I am wondering how people prove
themselves to be better than other people
by taking everything they have and then taking
what's left. I have nothing of my father's.
And without my mother's
filigree necklace, without her cape,
without a single picture, I cannot
prove who I am. Who would believe
a half-drowned stray? One of the maids
says, "Miss Louisa used to be
the smartest lady I ever met.
These spells are such a shame. But
the doctors can't find a cause."

The other maid sniffs. "A few weeks ago,
I caught her burying the cutlery
in the flower beds. And just yesterday,
she was hanging half outside the window
in this blasted cold, singing. She said she was
singing to the birds. Can you imagine?"

I can.
I catch my breath, hold it, let it go. I do not ask
if the birds sang back.

Sweeping Out the Hearth

I am covered in soot
when the coachman appears
out of nowhere, like Briarcliff
itself. He grabs a hunk of cheese
and knot of bread and escapes
through the back door, leaving me
to hope he didn't see me,
and to hope
he did.

Falling

The snow falls again the day after that, and
the day after that, snow enough to engulf

a castle. The temperature drops, locking us in.
Only the maids seem dismayed. At meals,

Arabella leans close to Paul Darbonne, hangs
upon his every word: "Is Darbonne a French

name? How do you pronounce it? Your family
imports teas and spices? How exciting!" She may

as well be squealing *Are you rich? You must be
rich!* How *rich?* Lucille bangs on the piano until

Aunt Louisa begs for a moment of silence.
She celebrates the fallen arches that kept

Mr. Darbonne from the war, then thrusts out
an arm. "My bracelet! Who took it?"

Paul Darbonne brings Aunt Louisa a cup
of hot tea, turns his amber eyes to me:

"Do you need help with that tray, Miss Bird?
Allow me, please." Outside the frosted window,

the coachman strips off his coat, rolls up shirtsleeves.
He hefts an axe and, with a single blow, splits a log

in two, his hair and shoulders sugared
with newly fallen snow.

Arabella

. . . is beautiful
even when she spits,
        "Stay away
from Paul Darbonne."
She grabs your wrist,
twists. "He feels nothing
but sorry for you."

A tiny flame bursts to life
inside you. You wrench your arm
from her sticky grip.

"Miss Louisa is *my* aunt.
My family."

Arabella's scoff
is the screech of a hawk,
the shriek of a kestrel.

"Tell her, then. Tell everyone.
They won't believe you.

And she won't remember you
tomorrow."

Princes

Once upon a time, I died.
        —Wait. Not me. My mother.
I was four. She was kind and beautiful

        in the way of mothers. (*Some*
mothers.)

        When Father was away,
Mother would set aside her silks,
        pull on plain cotton
                instead. We would share a ride
                on the back of her stallion, Red, chase
                        butterflies
                and gather flowers, shout at Herut the hound
                when she would try to kiss the
        bees. Scour
                the edges of our property for wild berries,
pick
        one for our baskets,
one for our bellies, till both were
        full.

Later, in the kitchen,
she and Cook would
mix the dough and
roll it thin
for pies. They would sip wine, giggle like children.
And then Mother would sing.

Mother's songs held more stories than Father's
whole library—stories of girls turned into rivers,
stories of girls turned into trees,
stories of girls who saved
little brothers, stories of girls
with magic
and wings.

Sometimes, in her stories, the girls
would marry kings
or princes.
I would ask her:
"What if a girl wants to be
the prince?"

She said I would understand
when I was older.
That I would find my prince like she found
my father.

On Fridays, she lit the candle and waved
three times, sang some more: *Baruch atah Adonai . . .*
At night,
she let me sleep in her room, my hand in her hand, my nose
nestled in her long curling hair,
dark hair that smelled of spices,
the names of which I didn't know.

(Cinnamon, orange peel, cardamom, clove.)

When I woke up in the middle
of the night,
twitching
over dreams of some witch, or some little
bother, she said, *Hush, hush,*
zeeskeit. I will never let the witch

catch you.

But it was she who was caught
by a cough
and a raging fever that would not let her go, even when
she crawled out onto the roof in the middle
of winter
to cool her blood.

My father said she turned into
an angel. But on the morning of her funeral

I woke up to a songbird
perched
in the branches of the old oak tree
next to my room, singing, singing.

Smoke and Butter

I pull on my coat and gloves and slip
out the kitchen door, though I do not know
where I am going. Someone shoveled a path
through the snow, and I follow it off the face
of the earth. It delivers me to the stables instead.

The soft snorts of the horses call to me, familiar
as songs my mother sang long ago. I open the door.
Inside, it is impossibly warm. In the nearest stall,
an enormous gray-black horse bobs his head, licks
his lips. I wish for an apple, a carrot, something
to feed him. I have nothing.

"What are you doing here?"

I spin around. Behind me, the coachman stands
so still I think he might be a ghost. "I was
trying to . . . escape."

"My specialty," he says. "But we won't get far
in this snow. His name is Smoke,
because he breathes fire."

"So, he's a magical horse," I say.

"All horses are magical," says the coachman. He digs
in his pocket, holds out cubes of sugar. "These are
Smoke's favorite. And Butter's, too." He pats the nose
of a palomino just as big as Smoke, but placid as the surface
of a pond.

I feed Smoke a few cubes of sugar, then Butter.
"Did you name them?"

"Aye. And raised them both.
The name's Duncan."

"I'm Bird."

"I remember," he says. "Birds
are magical, too."

"Some are," I say, a flush rising
in my cheeks, though
I don't know why.

"Are you going to tell me
how you ended up working
for that whiny lot?"

I am not. Butter rests her head
on my shoulder. "I miss
horses."

Duncan sweeps the cap from his head.
In this light, his hair is nearly black;
his eyes are a rich, dark blue, deeper
than a twilight sky. "I'd say they
miss you, too. Maybe we
could take a ride."

"I couldn't," I say. "I can't."

He takes a step closer and I must
tilt my head back to see. He's not as pretty
as Paul Darbonne, but something about him—
the jut of his jaw, the smell of leather and hay—
undoes me, my ribs like stays unwinding.

"My stepmother wouldn't approve."

"Your *stepmother*?" he says.
"That lot's your *family*?"

I shake my head no, but he's already
backing away.

On My Way Back to the House

A cardinal lands upon a tree branch
bristled
with fresh ice. She fluffs
red-brown wings, sings
her favorite song: *"Teeoo,*
who it, who it, who it?"

And I sing along with her,
but I don't know what she asks
and I don't know

the answer.

The Velvet Cape

The things you tell yourself:
That you might be allowed a seat
at the table after
serving.

That you might be allowed a glass
of wine, or a cup of Paul Darbonne's
imported tea, that your best

blue dress will do.

That you do not care about magic
horses or the coachman who loves
them.

That you are good enough
for any prince or aunt or
stepmother.

When you enter the parlor,
you do not expect
Arabella
draped in your mother's red
velvet cape, the carmine color so
jarring and so wrong
against
her mushroom skin.

Aunt Louisa's Raccoon Is Concerned Again

. . . and so is Aunt Louisa. She blares at me,

"Are you all right, dear?" I long to say, *Please*
ask your raccoon to tear my mother's

cape from Arabella's thieving back. But Paul
Darbonne is taking the empty teacup

from Aunt Louisa's hand and pouring her
some more. Not even the doctors

know what is causing her spells, but maybe
I do. I offer to take the cup

to Aunt Louisa, and smile as Darbonne's
fingers brush mine. When

no one is watching, I swap the cup with
Arabella's. My stepsister smirks

and smooths the velvet cape before
she takes a sip.

Kindling

I think about my mother, giggling
with Cook in the kitchen. I think about her

stories about girls with songs and girls
with wings, all those girls with their princes

and kings. What if *I* am the prince?
What if *I* am the king? But I don't want

to be anyone other than myself, Zipporah—
Bird—my mother's daughter,

her *zeeskeit*. I like cooking in the
kitchen; I like running with dogs

and horses. I like the smell of freshly
split wood and fire.

Fire

As if I conjured him
        myself,

Duncan sweeps into the room,
        arms piled with firewood, hair
        crowned with frost.

Burn

I pour a glass of wine for myself. I thank
        my aunt Louisa, my father's sister, for her

hospitality. Shock on Duncan's face, recognition on
Aunt Louisa's. Stepmother and my stepsisters protest

all at once, claim I'm a grim and greedy orphan
seeking to rob a feeble old woman of her fortune.

I say, "Your protests are quite rich, considering Paul
Darbonne's been drugging her. And you've been

helping him steal." Arabella attempts to sit upon a chair,
but misses the seat entirely and falls instead upon

the floor. She reaches up to Duncan so that he might help
her to her feet. But all he does is slip off the gold-

and-ruby bracelet she'd been wearing underneath
my mother's cape. He returns this to Aunt Louisa,

but she waves him off, eyes sharp and bright. "Give that
cape and bracelet to Bird. I believe red is her color."

After

Aunt Louisa turns the thieves out
into the cold, but not before we search rooms
and trunks, empty pockets. We find earrings
and brooches, cutlery and silver
serving platters, three sets of candlesticks,
a purse jangling with coins. Around Stepmother's neck,
under her fur collar,
a filigree necklace, shaped
like an outstretched hand, cradling
a diamond. My mother's hamsa. As the four
trudge away, a cardinal swoops and dives, pecks
their faces raw. Red tears stain the snow,

but I still refuse
to cry.

We Are the Briar

The moon spilling its luminous milk over
the hills and the river. My mother's ward,

her hamsa, around my neck and an aunt now
like a mother. A house, a castle, that gathers

itself when it wants to. A prince, no prince,
who prefers horses to business or tuxes. A man

with a name that sounds like the beating of
hooves, of hearts, on the lips. A kiss with

a promise of spring, of summer. More kisses.
Smoke and Butter. I am a maid like every

other, sweeping the hearth and tending to
supper, my life a song sung by a cardinal—

Who it who it who it—we are it and it is us.

Not So Sweet (an Anti-Cupid Story)

By Melanie Crowder

I.

It was a bad idea to land
in the perp lineup
outside the principal's office
on the Friday before
the sugared-up
school-day holiday
that is
Valentine's Day.

Everybody knows
the teachers' already grim
smiles grimace, stretch thin
by the end of *this* day—
what with the Cupidgrams
and hallway crush,
the Sweethearts Dance
and all that pheromone-jacked
locker-smash
teenage romance.

In hindsight,
the cotton-fluff angel wings
were also
a bad idea.

Like, who in their right mind
thought I would end up anywhere

but here, waiting
with some dumb-ass wings
strapped to my shoulders?
I couldn't even lean back
and fake that
juvie/punk
don't care/too cool
for everyone
and everything
thing.

There is nothing
remotely
cool
about me
today.

II.

On the cheap,
Kool-Aid is the way
to dip-dye the tips
of sun-bleached
summer hair.

Not your whole head.
    (Bad idea no. 3.)
Not when a long,
slushy winter
has stripped every last glimmer,
left it limp, lackluster,
not-summer-sun-
kissed.
Not any
kind of kissed.

Red no. 40 sugar crystals
ground my scalp gritty.
Itchy.
[bitchy]

It seemed like a good idea
at the time—cherry red
is the color of love. Also
of the angry coals
of a stamped-out
used-to-be
love.

III.

Hannah.

It's a sigh
more than a word.
Too tired from the parade of perps
to even speak my name.

Principal Shinn eyes
the glitzy-gold
pipe-cleaner halo
zinging
off a plastic headband
above my oh-so-red
head.

You ditched classes all day
only to show up like this?

Just getting into the holiday spirit?

My voice is a question
at the end,
mostly wincing, not
convincing anyone.

His eyes narrow, flicking
to the diamond glitter
bow and arrow
on his desk.

We have a zero-tolerance policy
when it comes to weapons,
young lady.

I don't know if we'd call that toy
a weapon, would we?

We would.

But the arrows aren't tipped! See?
They're plungers.

(Tiny plungers
for the toilet dwellers
who used to be my friends.)

I was just delivering
Cupidgrams.

Well,
Anti-Cupid
grams.

He unrolls the note
taped to the shaft

of the not-arrow,
the one that says
what Abigail said
Emory did
last summer
while Bea
was out of town.

Principal Shinn's
eyebrows lift,
lips thin.

Hannah.

His voice is stone.
Not sighing
anymore.

What
Were
You
Thinking?

I didn't do *it—*
Emory did.
I didn't say *it—*
Abigail did.

Though,
I've said it now,
I suppose.

I flinch,
cringe.

I didn't even shoot *the arrows*
(if you can call them that).
I mean,
I tried.

But like I said—
plastic dollar-store toy.
Not weapon.
Not projectile.
Not zero-toleranceable.

I slouch,
squirm.

Sigh.

So you are telling me
that words
cannot be shaped
into weapons?

IV.

The thing is,
I loved Jaime,
like, loved with the dreamy-eyed
luuuuuhhhvvvv
that would have gushed
and giggled
over a Cupidgram
on Valentine's Day.

Those golden eyes
and burnished lips,

his wicked smile spilling
secrets, spilling all
of the he-said
she-said,
even
(or maybe especially)
when he was behind-the-back
dishing
about one of our friends.

I didn't mind his wickedness
so long as it was my time
in the sun,
so long
as that scorch/sizzle
smile was all
mine.

But last Friday,
Jaime dumped me
for another girl
in our crew.

To split, then pick
from one of us
left a rift,
a had-to-be
shift:

her or me.

Somebody
had to go.

I should have known.

No one would turn their back
to that shimmer,
that bliss/burn
glow.

V.

I'd seen it before:
a breakup,
then a shake-up.
One used-to-be friend
cut loose.
It was cruel
but not one of us
said a damn thing.

Now that Jaime picked Bea
our whole crew
picked them
and nobody
picked
me.

VI.

I might have survived
the agony of a first love
        lost
but Bea was my friend,
I thought.

That kind
of sharp
stab

hits bitter,
stomach gone sour,
spoiled,

sad.

But they say revenge
is sweet,
so I thought instead
of what would hurt
her
and him
and all of them
instead of me.

VII.

I skipped school,
armored up in tinsel wings,
a bedazzled bow,
and painted hair.
On eight notes
I wrote a bit of that he-said,
she-said,
wrapped each arrow shaft
in the sting
of buried secrets
aired.

Maybe I needed the whole day
to prepare.

More like
I was scared to face

this love-encrusted day
all day.

The whole crew together
and me—
not-gushing
not-giggling
not-together
ing.

I rolled up right
before the last bell
for the last class
to empty hallways
and closed doors.

A plastic bowstring
can't sling anything
across the hall.
Arrow no. 1 slip-flopped
to the floor,
not-heroic,
not-romantic,
too close to the mark
of pathetic
for my liking.

So I closed a fist
over the shaft and plunged
one arrow after another
onto my ex-friends'
lockers, all
stabby-swagger
anti-Cupid
glower
almost-power.

Eight lockers,
shafts quivering,
notes dangling.

Eight used-to-be friends.
Eight used-to-be secrets.

Revenge is sweet,
I whispered.

You don't get
to just drop
me.

The bell squealed,
squeezing between chinks
in my not-so-strong
armor.

Anger fizzled
into squishier
underbelly-er
kinds of feelings
I'd rather not
feel.

VIII.

The hallway filled,
spilled over
with *luuuuuhhhvvvv.*

I could have left—
but I didn't.

I wanted to see them
unfriended,
like me,
uneasy.

I wanted them to know
there was no
pretending
they hadn't hurt
me.

Time slowed,
one target approached
and the next
then the next
and the next,
all together, all
cheeks pinked,
lips parted,
openhearted.

Delayed reaction,
gut-punch titters,
curtained hands, oh-so-harsh
whispers.
Wicked glee, cackle/laugh
each of my arrows
in someone else's
back.

One by one,
they unfurled
my Anti-Cupidgrams.

Not one
giggle left.

Cheeks pinked,
lips parted,
brokenhearted.

Angry words,
barbed tips
found their targets.

IX.

Principal Shinn is not impressed.

> *Has it occurred to you, Hannah,*
> *that people who abandon you*
> *because of a breakup*
> *do not make*
> *the best kind of friend*
> *material*
> *in the end?*
>
> *Of course,*
> *I can't think of anyone*
> *who'll be thinking you*
> *are any kind of friend*
> *material*
> *after the stunt*
> *you pulled*
> *today.*

A three-day suspension,
parental consternation,
seven Saturdays
of community service,
and a sticky stain
on my college applications.

What
Was
I
Thinking?

Turns out the slow trudge
out of the principal's office
is worse
than the perp lineup
ever was.

X.

My not-crew
waits for me outside
under a mean February sun.

Revenge is sweet,
I remind myself.

But even unspoken
the words wobble
waver
wilt.

There they wait,
tearstained
cheeks inked,
eyes glitter-glare.

                    Nice wings,
Bea says.

My arrow in her fist.
Her note ripped to bits.

Snap.
A splintered shaft
drops at my feet.

Sweet hair.
Emory's voice cuts, plastic
sarcastic.

Snap.

Cherry-red sweat slides,
slip/drips
in my eyes;
they sting, well,
sharp tears
swell.

Cute bow.
Titter/snort.

Snap.

Four more arrows
hit the ground.
Not-scorned smiles
from the not-sorry
sorry excuses
for used-to-be
(bonding in shared disdain of me)
friends.

They walk away,
arms linked,
shared last laugh;
no last look
back.

Apparently,
the best kind
of friend material
is a common enemy.

It's easier
than the squishier
underbelly-er
kinds of feelings
they'd rather not
feel.

XI.

It's just me now
and that mean sun
and some frosty
February air.

Just me.

I wish I liked
what I see;
all I see
is me, bruised
and bruising,
violet blooming under
too-thin skin.

I think—

I think maybe falling in
with that crew
was my first
bad idea.

I think maybe secrets
are no kind of
currency—not for me.
Not for the kind of friend
I think
I'd like to try
to figure out how
to be.

See,
if revenge *is* sweet,
it's the artificial
Red no. 40
burn your own eyes out
kind—

not for me,
I think,

really not
so sweet
at all.

The Bridegroom's Oak

By Kip Wilson

Germany, 1899

Escape

The work day crawls
to an end with each
        tick
each
        tock
animating me, making me
itchy to run
from the drudgery
of metallic
        clunks
        clacks
        whirrs
of the machine in front of me,
needle flying over cloth
like a bird
over patchwork fields
outside of town.

How I long to fly like that.

Not Too Quickly, Now

The clock chimes six
I push back my chair
get to my feet

try not to trample
the other girls in a rush
for the door.

Magda and Erna are bookends
twenty-year-old twins
        two years older than us
whose identical movements
I can picture
twenty years from now
in this same town
in this same dressmaker's shop
        (more hunched, more faded,
        but still here)

while Gretchen, dear Gretchen,
crouches quiet, soft, twitchy indoors,
only to burst outside
                and bloom.

Fresh Air

Out of doors
Gretchen and I
                exhale
locking
        arms, hasten
our step, rush
                out
        of town and
                        into
                the forest.

As soon as we set foot
among the trees

towering tall as kings,
our pace slows
our breathing calms
our minds relax.

We're free, Lotte! Gretchen's words
a whoosh of air. *I couldn't wait
to get out of there today.*

I know what you mean,
I say, because of course I do
and we skip, twirl, take in
this sanctuary.

Dreams

We daydream of
escape
not simply away
from here but
toward
the city of light

saving our coins
to take us to
the world capital
of *maisons de couture*
the center of the fashion magazines we devour
Paris.

Playing Pretend

Gretchen and I have been sneaking off to
the forest to study last season's magazines
from the shop since we began working there

four years ago at age fourteen and
our conversations always begin the same way:
Imagine if . . .
followed by dreams
of what it would be like to share
a garret, work in Paris.

Today I begin, *Imagine if*
one of our own dresses
winds up in a magazine,
perhaps even on the cover?

Gretchen continues, *Imagine if*
we wind up celebrated by
designers, shopkeepers, customers?

A snap of a twig,
a pause, followed by
a deep, decidedly male voice:
Imagine if
an old friend designs
new creations for you
but instead of cloth
they're made of chocolate?

I startle, freeze, whip around
to face the young man who walked
into our daydream
uninvited.

Mysterious

Werner Waldschmidt
our former classmate (back when we still went to school)
stands before us.

Excuse me, but I don't think
we asked your opinion.
I arch an eyebrow
launch a look his way
while my insides warm
    remembering.

Hurt and shame rise up pink
over Werner's face, sending
the tiniest twinge of guilt
through my heart.

I can't help taking in
his charming face
framed with thick chestnut hair
dotted with chocolate eyes
    dark as the fancy confections
    from his family's factory.

I clear my throat, look away
as Gretchen tugs
on my elbow because
she knows as well as I do

that this particular boy
is strictly
off-limits.

Old Stories

Gretchen takes it one step further,
telling Werner he's not welcome, and
he takes off like
a startled young buck
dashing away from

a hunter's rifle
        leaves fluttering
                in his wake.

My gaze wistfully follows
the path Werner took
toward his home (lovely as a gingerbread house)

but Gretchen clears her throat
gaze reproachful.

                                You know you aren't supposed
                                to speak to him.

She knows very well
that I know.

And yet
that hair
those eyes
sweet as the treats his family creates,
which I've never been lucky enough to taste.

And yet that question
                Why?
or is it
                Why not?
still burns in my heart.

Sunset

The next evening after another long work day
Gretchen and I flit once again
through the forest until it's time
to head back to our homes.

On the way, we pass
my favorite tree, set apart
from all the others
in the forest
        tall
        strong
        regal
a towering oak
that welcomes me to
its feet like a loving grandfather.

But something makes me look up
to a knot above my head where
I spy a slip of paper poking out
in the darkening evening

and I reach for that scrap of paper
hide it in my palm
read it silently.

Three Little Lines

Do you still remember that day too?
Our eyes meeting, fingertips brushing,
that moment full of possibility?

Secret

My cheeks flame with heat.
Of course I remember.

But I never told anyone
        not even Gretchen

so when I flip the note over to find a sketch of a girl
dark curls escaping a heavy bun atop her head

and a spray of freckles over her cheeks—
a girl who looks very much like me

I cover her with my hand and silently slip
the paper back in the knot.

Reflection

I steal a glance at Gretchen
and her eyes are moons.

What is it? she whispers.

It's nothing.
I shake my head

because we both know
nothing
will get in the way
of our future
of Paris

not even my
long-dormant feelings for
this boy.

Home

It's gotten late
we must speed home

to the chores, supper, families
that await

but after Gretchen turns
toward her own farmhouse

with a promise to spend
Saturday evening together

I don't hesitate. I rush back
to my oak to retrieve that slip of paper and

reading those three lines again makes my
heart beat even faster as I race for home.

My Dear Mother

Face careworn with lines
hair streaked with gray
Mutti has had a hard life
and I know better
than to ask
why
she's forbidden
contact with Werner:
the town's rumor mill continues
to churn the tale that she
was one of two girls his father courted.

The Kindest Father

My own Vati was a farmer,
a kind, gentle man
who scooped Mutti

up from her despair
        (or so they say)

who offered her flowers and
fruit trees instead of
chocolates

who set her up in
this sweet cottage
between the edge of the forest
and the edge of our fields

but whose kind heart
couldn't bear the strain
of his efforts anymore
and one day
simply stopped
        ticking.

Hermit

I don't know what
Mutti was like as a girl
but I do know
what she's been like
since Vati died

quiet and caring
to me and my brothers
(ten-year-old Oskar and eight-year-old Otto)
but averse—even afraid—of contact
with anyone else in town

content to stay
in our cottage, our fields,

not trusting the world
that lies beyond
the apple trees.

A Burning Hole

Through the darkening evening,
I place my hand over my apron pocket
once, twice, three times,
anxious to read the words again
yet just as anxious to keep
them secret from
everyone else.

I finally get my moment
when Mutti steps out to the
barn to milk the cow
while the boys stack wood
beside the fireplace.

By the light of the candle
I commit those words on
paper to memory, wondering
for the first time if
love
ought to be higher
on an eighteen-year-old girl's list
than adventure.

Nighttime Worries

After supper, cleanup,
stories I tell my brothers,
I try to get to sleep

but when I lie in my bed
first thinking of Paris
then thinking of Werner

my mind whirs nonstop
eventually coming to rest
neither on Paris nor love

but on the family I'd leave
behind either way
if I followed my heart.

Feierabend

On Saturday
after the clock chimes six
Gretchen and I can't get
out of doors quickly enough.

We brush past
        Magda and Erna
for our regular walk
through the woods
and I scurry toward the oak
        my oak

which has sat absent
of additional notes
but which today
                finally
holds another slip of paper
sticking out of the familiar knot
like a postal box.

My breath catches in my throat

as I continue on the path
beside Gretchen until she turns,
reminding me,

I'll be over after
I get my bag from home.

I wave, wait,
before rushing back to my oak.

A Poem

Seeing you the other day
reminds me of all I want to say

that despite being forbidden
I can't keep my feelings hidden

so if you turn around
your future could be found

in the day's last light
hidden in plain sight.

A Mystery

I whirl around
as if expecting
to see Werner Waldschmidt
standing right there
behind me

but not a twig snaps
not a leaf bends.

I look over the words again.

The day's last light, I whisper.

Of course! When you stand at the edge
of the forest facing our cottage
the sun sets behind the hill before you.

I race through the forest
toward home and the setting sun,
and when I arrive
at the border of my family's land
a figure emerges.

It's Werner

The smile on my face must
match his, which grows
larger as I approach.

Is it from you? I ask,
holding up the note
like a challenge.

Guilty as charged. He smiles,
hair floppy, cheeks pink.
I've tried my best to forget
but I can't hide my feelings
any longer simply because
someone else demands it.

I wince
remembering another
pivotal moment between us

when I told him
I couldn't see him
ever again.

A Gift

Werner reaches
in his coat pocket, extracts
a small shape wrapped
in brown paper, and
my fingers tremble
as I accept the package
unwrap the most lovely
chocolate rose.

I bring it to my lips, let
the smooth flavor slide
down my tongue,
tasting equally
        bitter
        and
        sweet.

Betrayal

A rustling behind me, a throat clearing,
Werner's hand raised in greeting
to someone behind me. I turn.

Lotte. Gretchen clutches a satchel
over her shoulder and a handful of
sunflowers to her chest, awkwardly
stepping backward. *Werner?*

She says his name
like an accusation
laced with disapproval

and before I can respond
she's dropped the flowers
and disappeared.

Choices

The best friend
running away from me
or the boy standing behind me

and I can only choose one.

Spellbound

I turn back around and
Werner's there in front of
me, closer than ever.

It's as though I'm under
some sort of a spell
in which it isn't enough
to taste his chocolate
perhaps even crafted
with his own hands

and after a moment of hesitation
I take one last step
    closing
    the distance
    between us

until there's nothing
keeping us apart.

Clang!

From across the field
our cow's bell breaks
the moment in half.

Werner and I fly
apart like that bell
is a gunshot

which it might as well be
when I see Mutti charging
after the cow toward us.

Fury

Over the years
I've seen Mutti
    content
    sad
    determined

but I've never seen her
so angry that
she couldn't even speak.

She points
to me, to the house
to Werner, to the forest
and the two of us have no choice
but to go our separate ways.

Facing My Punishment

Otto and Oskar are playing
with sticks in the yard
and I brush past them
with a warning.
Best stay out here for a while.

As soon as I'm inside
I attempt to make
myself useful, stoking
the fire, setting the table.

Mutti enters
like a storm cloud
dark and powerful.
She points me to sit, paces furiously
hands balled in fists
until she finally deflates.

Story Time

Mutti slumps into
the chair across from me
runs a hand over her hair
her cheeks pale as moonlight.

I do my best to make amends.
I'm sorry.

She sighs. *I'm sorry, too.*
It's not really about the boy.
It wasn't then, either.
Back with Werner's father.

Walter Waldschmidt passed away far too soon
        the same year as
        my own father.

He might have tempted me
with chocolates and kisses, but
as soon as I saw the way she
looked at him, I stepped aside.
Mutti pauses.
Marta Waldschmidt.
        Werner's mother.
We were the best of friends.
Like you and your Gretchen.

I freeze. I never knew
Mutti had a best friend
        or a friend at all.
I blink, confused.

When Werner married Marta
        she chose him, leaving me
behind. Another pause.
I promise you
if you choose romance
                over friendship
you'll regret it.

A tear rolls down her cheek
as she mourns not him
                but *her*

and suddenly
        everything
becomes clear, including
my own situation.

The Longest Night

I wake in the wee
morning hours from
a fitful sleep
filled first with dreams of Werner
and his chocolates and kisses
followed by nightmares of
Gretchen left behind
as the earth quakes, cracks,
opens a divide between us two.

It's still dark
I'm still exhausted
when the day begins
    my brothers up for school
    me for work
    Mutti to rustle us
        out of the house.

I rub my eyes mechanically
do my morning chores
while I wonder if there's a way
to avoid choosing.

The Longest Morning

Once at work, I'm unable to concentrate
on my stitches, making several mistakes
before the noon bells chime.

Gretchen looks my way.
We should talk. How about
some fresh air over lunch?

I nod, avoiding her gaze,
my insides knotted up
with anxiety and guilt.

We pull on our coats
pick up our packages of Butterbrot
head outside, where

despite the hazy sunshine,
it's colder than it looked
through the windows.

We wordlessly munch
our bread as we wander our tiny town
where everyone knows everyone.

Gretchen speaks first.
Are you and Werner . . . ?
Her voice trails off.

I press my lips together
unsure whether to acknowledge my feelings
unwilling to hurt hers.

But Gretchen takes
my lack of denial as an admission
her face clouding over.

This is all so . . .
Gretchen searches for the
right word . . . *sudden.*

It isn't anything at all, not really,
I say, *and even if it were,*
you'd always be my best friend.

We'll see.
Gretchen avoids my gaze
like she doesn't believe me.

My jaw clenches.

You sound just like Werner's mother
ready to ruin a friendship
by making assumptions!

My mother didn't miss
him
but her*!*

I whirl back around toward work
only to find Frau Waldschmidt herself
behind me

hand over mouth
realization
filling her horror-stricken eyes.

Moment of Reckoning

My cheeks flame
as I speed past Werner's mother
a woman
I've not spoken to
my entire life

but I feel her gaze burn
into my back
even as Gretchen's feet
pound after mine
even as I retrace our

walk back to the shop
even as I wonder, breathless,
what that woman
and what my best friend
        must both be thinking.

Daily Drudgery

Gretchen appears
        deep in thought
as she settles in next to me
back at our worktable
for our long afternoon
filled not with gossip
but instead
with the metallic
        clunks
        clacks
        whirrs
of the machines
in front of us all.

Soon I'm swept away
not by my thoughts or
worries but by the
fabric and thread coming
together under my fingers.

My Best Friend

When the clock chimes
the end of day, I avoid
Gretchen and her silence
prepare to make my way

into the forest
        alone if I must.

For a moment I even
forget her completely as
against all advice I imagine
the familiar knot in my oak tree
        my breath hitching
        at the hope that
a new note might be
waiting for me

but when I follow everyone
gathering up their things,
it's a surprise to find
        Gretchen
waiting at the door for me.

Surprise

Magda and Erna scatter
and Gretchen reaches
for my arm.

It probably doesn't matter now,
but I have to tell you something.
She clears her throat.
I wrote to a couple
of the maisons de couture
in Paris to see if any are taking on
        apprentices.

I raise an eyebrow.

maisons de couture?
Which ones?

The House of Worth.
The House of Paquin.

Two of the houses
mentioned again and again
in our fashion magazines.

I received a response from
Jeanne Paquin herself yesterday.
If we can get ourselves there
by the end of the month,
two apprenticeships await.

The life in Paris
we had planned together

so different from a life here
even one that includes a chocolatier.

A wave of regret
washes over me.

Not only did I make
my own assumptions
about Gretchen,
but she remains the one
dedicating herself to
the future of our friendship

and I finally undeniably realize
chocolate eyes
and chocolate confections
notwithstanding

where my true loyalty
and my dreams should lie.

The Light at the End

I slip my arm
through Gretchen's, lead
the way through the forest.

I might hold certain feelings
for a certain boy,
    but
long as I might live,
I'll never find a truer friend than you.
I'll ask Mutti if we might go
as we always dreamed
    to the city of light
        Paris.

The Future Is Now

Gretchen gasps with joy
    smile stretching wide
        as she skips through the forest,
and I'm so pleased to follow her
        that I don't even spare
    my oak a glance
as we pass it by.

Family

The last stumbling block
isn't even facing Werner

to share my decision
but
                Mutti
        Otto and Oskar
people I don't want
to leave behind.

Still, I plan to reassure them
about what this move will mean
hopeful they'll agree that
Paris is the best place for me.

A Visitor

I arrive home to find
not only Mutti and
my brothers as usual
but also
        a woman
at our table, her back
to the door.

I freeze at the threshold
my mind a blank
and
an explosion of thought
all at once.

The woman turns and
Mutti speaks, her words warm.

Lotte, meet Frau Waldschmidt.
Marta, my daughter, Lotte.

I scan Mutti's face
but instead of
anxiety
displeasure
or even
annoyance

all I detect is delight.

It's a pleasure, Lotte.
Frau Waldschmidt beams.

I can't even think
how to respond
not even
when the two of them
share a glance
burst into a giggle.

You've reconciled?
I barely dare whisper.

I foolishly thought your mother was
jealous, Frau Waldschmidt says.
If I'd only known it was me
she missed . . .

It'll take a while to make up
for lost time, Mutti says, *but*
we've already rekindled our
friendship this afternoon.

They smile and embrace
clinging to each other like
precious memories come to life.

I nod furiously.
I can't believe I almost made
the same mistake.

I proceed to share
the good news
about Gretchen and me
our invitation to Paris
our apprenticeships
our dream

and these two women
who haven't spent as much
as a moment together
in all the years I've been alive
squeal
clap their hands

simply thrilled
at this completed circle
of girlhood friendship.

Shooting Stars

That night, after
eating supper
finishing chores
reading a story
Mutti and I tuck
the boys in bed, step
into the yard, look
up at the night sky.

I'll miss you, of course, but
what a wonderful adventure.

A shiny star shoots
from where it's hanging
over the trees toward
the Earth below.

Make a wish!

For a moment
my thoughts sweep
to that boy with
    chocolate eyes
    and chocolate treats

but I close my eyes, wish
that my life in Paris fulfill
    my wildest dreams
in an adventure that will seal
a bond to my best friend
no one will ever
    break.

Author's Note

This story was inspired by the Bridegroom's Oak—an actual tree in the Dodauer Forest in Eutin, Germany—and the first young couple who secretly exchanged letters there in 1891. They married beside the tree, which continues to serve as a public mailbox for lovers to this day.

La sirena y el zemí

By Margarita Engle

1. La sirena speaks

Human storytellers have always
misunderstood merfolk.

Las sirenas sing to attract winged spirits,
not featherless sailors on fragile boats.

We are daughters of Atabey,
ruler of moonlight, tides, rivers,
islands, and oceans . . .

We dance atop waves
to entice flying sprites
even though we
are seabound,
unable to soar.

Our home is in the depths
where stone pyramids and crowded cities
sank long ago, after the sea level rose
enough to submerge a land bridge
between Yucatán and Cuba.
We have no gills, so we have to swim
to the surface
every few hours,
filling our lungs
with sky

and our eyes
with visions
of wings
flying
high above,
as if los zemís
were birds
made especially
for us.

Humans imagine that merfolk breathe like fish,
but the truth is, we're more like whales,
deep divers who know how to hold
precious air.

Whenever los seres humanos catch us,
they trap us in tanks
and treat us like pets.

In captivity, we suffer loneliness,
swimming round and round
like hopeless goldfish

in bowls . . .

but I'm free now
and each time I rise toward sunlight
I see los zemís, the winged guardians
of fields, forests, streams, ponds, and springs.

Nose above water,
I inhale their scent
of blossoms and moss
from a leafy green jungle.

It's the fragrance
of ancestral memory
reminding me how easily
my ancestors moved on land
and in flowing water
and windy air.

My father is a river spirit.
Los zemís are his servants.
I am not my parent's equal,
but I do not
care.

Some of the muscular winged spirits
are deep blue or rainforest green
with tangled hair that looks
like roots
or vines,
but the special zemí
who sees me clearly
is reddish brown
like a copper coin
tossed down to waves
by people on ships,
men, women, and children
who imagine that merfolk
can grant gifts
in the form of pearls
and other treasures.

Now, with pelicans and gulls swarming around him,
el zemí meets my gaze, returning the true gift
of curiosity.

When he speaks,
his voice is music.

My own song begins and ends
with sighs of some emotion
I've never even tried
to imagine—love
the ultimate
wave.

Everyone knows there are moments so mysterious
that they cannot be ignored without losing
the beauty of a meant-to-be
future.

So I reach
and he lifts me
until we are both
soaring together,
carried by wind
and wings
and hope.

2. El zemí speaks

Falling in love with a sea being was not
my sunrise vision or moonlit dream.

All I wanted was a morning far away
from my own story.

As the guardian of la poza de los enamorados,
I live in a treetop above a mountain spring
where two lovers drowned long ago
while fleeing the girl's enraged father.

The boy was poor
and she was rich,

but both were mere humans with no way
to overcome their fear, no wings
or whale-deep lungs
for diving,
or any other source
of natural courage.

So they chose
the only path open to them—disappearance
followed by invisibility.

Now they live behind a waterfall
and they know I'll always protect them
in their spirit forms, but they always tell me
that I need love too.

Gazing down
at the blue-sky hair
and sea-green eyes
of this sirena,
I feel
enchanted.

Her voice
meets mine
and our melodies
intertwine.

Never before have I felt
such a height of wishing.

Our music asks wordless questions
about oceanic depths
and sky-touched
trees.

She lifts me
when I reach.

We fly
inland.

Heartbeats
and wingbeats
play the same rhythm,
a drummed song
of movement
from the solitary
past
to a hopefully
shared
                                        future.

We reach the plaza central of el pueblo
de la Santísima Trinidad, where Atabey rests
inside the smooth stone of a marble statue
that humans choose to call Terpsichore,
muse of choral singers
and dancers
and dreams.

Mother of mermaids.
She gives us her blessing.

Then we ask the same
of la sirena's father, who flows like rain
in el río Manatí.

We rise again, two wings enough
to lift paired spirits who both know
that our future cannot be defeated
by any human actions,

no matter how foolish,
selfish,
or ignorant.

If only they would listen
to our songs, the sea breeze
and my rhythm of dancing leaves,
peaceful nature always available
as the background for any real
or imagined
daydream.

Without her own wings
la sirena cannot enjoy life in a treetop,
so we move to the shore of the pool of lovers,
where we live between worlds
just like
humans.

Author's Note

This story was inspired by real places and real legends. The sunken pyramids are off the west coast of Cuba, and la poza de los enamorados is in the Sierra del Escambray, near my mother's hometown of Trinidad de Cuba, where a statue of Terpsichore seems compatible with my Indigenous Ciboney Taíno ancestors' stories about Atabey and her aquatic descendants.

Borrowed Blossoms

BY DAVID BOWLES

Mesoamerica, fifteenth century

Ninth Prince

Mecello

Being the ninth son
of the least powerful king
in the Triple Alliance of Anahuac,
I long ago learned to accept
whatever little privilege
and power I can get.

I hope one day to be made
Lord of Ceremonies,
overseeing music and dance
in Tlacopan, the city of my birth,
capital of Tepanecapan,
the least beloved third
of a growing empire.

So nothing prepares me
for my father's announcement:
"Mecello, precious jewel,
you will accompany me
to Tenochtitlan, transferring
to the imperial academy,
the Calmecac of Quetzalcoatl."

It is an honor reserved
for noble Mexica teens
or the crown princes of allies,
not for a consort's son
like me, youngest prince,
future functionary.

"Thank you, my royal father,
for such a gift to one so unworthy,"
I say as I kneel before him.
He pulls me to my feet.
"Just watch out for the enemy,
that Tlaxcalteca boy."

In a Strange Land

Omaca

So this is famed Tenochtitlan.
It's definitely big and pretty,
like an oversized gem set
in a thin spiral of silver—
easily broken and lost.

And I hate all the formalities.
The boring, aristocratic rituals
get on my nerves—in Tlaxcallan,
especially Tizatlan, my hometown,
what matters is your *worth*,
what you master, what you achieve.
My granddad went from farmer
to military hero, then taught that ethic
to both his sons. My uncle represents
our region on the governing council.

My dad's now a general,
commanding Tizatlan's army,
leading this diplomatic delegation
to seek true, lasting peace.

But the greetings finally end,
and the reception begins.
I just *love* the performances—
dozens of masked men dancing
to the sound of drums and flutes
and whistles, over which floats
sweet and strong the sound of a duet:
two mythic warriors, locked in battle,
singing their teary goodbyes
before slaying each other.

Music. It's all I care about.

Dad has brought me here
to attend the Mexica's calmecac,
an exclusive academy for nobles,
unlike our free and open schools.

"It's a sign of our trust and goodwill,
Omaca—and your chance to show
that we're not the barbarians
these arrogant bastards believe."
Dad pauses and leans closer.
"I also want you to keep an eye
on their princes. Learn what you can."

What *I want*, however, is to learn
the secrets of song from the bards,
legendary throughout the world,
that Mexica emperors hoard
like riches on this island.

Learning My Place

Mecello

Of the three kingdoms of which
the empire is comprised, ours—
Tepanecapan—is the least respected,
as many princes remind me.

I endeavor not to call attention to myself,
but some are determined to humiliate me,
such as Tlacaellel the Younger,
grandson of the prime minister.

"Your father," he says coldly during lunch,
"would undo the tradition of Flower Wars
that my grandfather, architect of the empire,
instituted to please the gods and ease famine."

"My good prince," I try to assure him,
"the king of Tepanecapan will do nothing
that would harm the Triple Alliance.
Nor would I, for that matter. Rest easy."

Tlacaellel looks around at the other boys
and laughs, a grim and ghoulish sound.
"There is no resting at this school, Mecello.
We will help you learn your place, little prince."

Misery Loves Company

Omaca:
It's bizarre to see a crown prince
get treated like shit, but the Mexica nobles
mostly harass him with words,

though once in a while he gets slapped
or shoved or tripped.

I know I shouldn't.
I know what Dad would say.
But every time he's down,
I reach out to help him up.

Ah, but Mecello can be an ass.
There's never gratitude in his eyes.
Just confusion pretending to be anger.

Mecello:
Most students wear their hair shorn.
Those who have seen battle, like me,
and have taken a single prisoner—
we get to grow a lock above one ear.
Novice warriors in their last year
can grow their hair to the jawline.

But the Tlaxcalteca barbarian
arrives with his hair in a braid
down his back like a girl.
It's striking—maybe lovely—
and wholly inappropriate.

The first thing the nobles do
when we're all alone in the Hall of Sleep
is hold him down on his mat near me
to slice and scrape it all away
with makeshift knives of flinty stone
while Omaca strives to break free
by twisting and kicking.

I don't want to pity him. But I must watch him.
I don't want to care. It's just my assignment.

The Routine

Omaca

Before the sunrise
strikes the sacred spring,
we spill a few drops
of our blood
to thank the gods
for their sacrifice,
which gave us light.

Morning prayers
and patio sweeping
before our classes,
fasting until noon.
Then a meager meal
of tortillas and beans
chock-full of chilis.

Daily dose of bullying,
then afternoon classes.
Martial arts. Weapons.
Then supper and more
sweeping, cleaning,
praying, and, at last,
singing all together
till bedtime comes.

But just as I start
to fall asleep on my mat,
the Master of Boys
awakens us to sweep
the patio again! (Mexica
love their gods-damned
sweeping, I swear.)

A little rest at last,
while a few students
rut quick in the dark,
then it all begins again.

New Arrivals

Mecello

Most of the students are scions
of the imperial family,
my distant cousins, but strangers
or acquaintances, at best,
whom I see but a few times a year.

So the austere life of noble teens—
the brief sleep, strenuous training,
ritual bleeding, meager meals—
is made even worse by hazing
and insults and cold shoulders.

None of it compares, of course,
with their treatment of Omaca.
Yet our shared predicament
renders us equally outsiders.

And when we practice music and dance
in the House of Song, I can't help but note
the fierce precision of his beats, the fluid
movement of his body, the raspy melodies
of his foreign tongue, all broad vowels and
breathy consonants, a highlander's voice.

I'm devoted to poetry. I can't resist its pull,
no matter whose heart it chooses to bloom in.

The Song Master notices,
and out of cruelty or kindness
assigns us a duet for debut,
underscoring our otherness.

"An Otomi hymn of spring,"
he says with a strange smile,
"for the new arrivals."

My eyes meet Omaca's
and he nods. We both
know the words by heart.

The Duet

Mecello and Omaca, drums and voices

"I enter that many-flowered land,
the realm of bliss and play
where glittering dew rains down,
and holy bells ring bright and clear.
Precious birds intone eternal songs,
their sweet voices bringing joy
to the Lord of the Near and the Nigh."

We step from behind the drums,
our feet slapping out the rhythm
as we repeat that line in refrain,
then bow and switch places
for the second verse.

"I follow that hymn to its source—
not on earth do melodies arise . . .
from heaven's bosom those notes fly!
Parrot, ibis, oriole:

They trill the sacred chants.
Ah! How they praise him there,
the Lord of the Near and the Nigh."

Now our dance weaves us
closer together, till we almost
touch as we croon the refrain
before our final verse.

"Behold! Such brightly colored singers,
once my companions on the battlefield,
now transformed and forever content
to follow the sun as he rises each day,
warbling his glory, flying side by side.
As I spread my wings in the House of Dawn,
I'll look for you, my brother and friend,
so we can set off together once more."

Our hands are still on the drums
while students hoot and howl.
Neither of us will soon forget
how perfectly our voices,
our hands, and our feet
just flowed together.

Night Whispers

Omaca:
"Are you okay, knave?
You cried out as if in pain
as you tossed and turned.

"Let me guess. Bad dreams
full of shitty noble boys."

Mecello:
"I'm fine, *Prince Omaca.*
Worry about your own fate.
I can handle my nightmares."

Omaca:
"Gods-damned noble brats.
Act like they're pure Mexica
when they're mutts like you and me."

Mecello:
"We are not alike.
I'm Tepaneca, through and through.
I want nothing to do with you."

Practice Bout #1

Mecello

The Mexica treat me
as a signal drummer,
unlikely to ever fight,
so when Captain Tizoc
pairs me with a youth
from Tlatelolco,
I show them precisely why
I am permitted to wear this lock
by knocking him flat
on his back.

I then see Omaca
squaring off against
Prince Huitzilatzin,
all bluster and bravado

though chubby and short,
looking like a snotty brat
four summers younger.

The Tlaxcalteca boy
is superior in every way,
but rather than take down
his opponent quickly,
he plays with him
as an ocelot might a rat—
taking his time,
showing us his skill.

I've never seen moves
quite like his before.
Then again, I've only
been in battle against
Chalca warriors. Once.
Tlaxcalteca martial arts
are a novelty. Watching,
I understand how Tlaxcallan
has remained undefeated.

When Omaca disarms Huitzilatzin at last,
he turns to Tlacaellel, smiling. "Next?"

Practice Bout #2

Omaca

Next I am paired with Mecello.
That thin, honey-eyed kid
has captured but never killed.

I want to disarm him quickly,
but his defense is a dance
full of joy and skill.

That rhythm is infectious.
Soon I'm dancing, too, as something
between us starts to build.

It's like we feel the same beat
thrumming just for him and me
in the earth beneath our feet.

Reflected in each other's eyes,
we pound our shields with wonder
till Captain Tizoc shrills.

"You're not courting, sweet princes!
Now attack or be punished."

But our swords remain still.

Punishment

Mecello:
The lashes do not faze me—
we're beaten face-to-face,
and my spirit thrills . . .

Omaca:
Despite the risk, Mecello smiles,
chanting in time with the blows:

Mecello:
"Like flowers that wilt,
friends are lent but for a while.

So enjoy them when they bloom:
Such is the gods' will."

Omaca:
The sound of his voice
and the last blow
soon fade into the dusk.

But inside me,
I think they'll echo
for many days and weeks.

Toilet Duty

Mecello

Omaca and I are assigned
the least dignified of duties.
Every morning we have to
empty chamber pots into a vat
and carry the waste far away
to the canal that separates
the sacred plaza from the rest
just as the sanitation barge
paddles by, helping to keep
the biggest city in the world
as clean as it can be.

When our age group awakens
in the middle of each night to
sweep the patio, feed the fires,
prick limbs with thorns to bleed
in ritual penance, they give us
a wide berth as if we're filthy.

So rather than remain silent,
respectfully focused,
Omaca and I talk.

And talk.
And talk.

Though racked by guilt,
I don't report his words.

They're only meant for me.

What We Have in Common

Omaca

We're the same height,
our skin the same ochre
as highland clay.

We're bad at playing ball,
embarrassingly bad.

But we're great at dancing,
like an axolotl, twisting freely
in a clear stream.

Our weakness? Turkey eggs.
We don't like chocolate much,
unless sweetened with honey.

Neither of us likes Mexica royalty,
all their revisionist history, elevating
barbarian invaders to chosen ones.

That's part of what helps us connect—
we're both outsiders, in our own way,
to the imperial culture of power.

We both prefer the haunting melodies
of Otomi music to the martial monotone
of nationalism that grips this island.

We both collect exotic instruments:
His favorite is a whalebone flute,
mine a copper drum from Cuextlan.

Our hands fit together
like two pieces of a puzzle.

And though we've lived our lives
near rivers and lakes, we both hope
to see western waves crashing
as the sun plunges into the ocean.

Skipping School

Omaca

Stupid rules. In my country,
adults must earn the respect
of peers and kids alike.

So on the sixth day
of hauling crap,
I make a suggestion.

"Mecello, you say you visit
this city often with your father.
It's like a second home.

"Well, we deserve a break!
Show me the sights and sounds
of the imperial capital."

He hesitates, eyes glinting
almost gold with the sunrise.
Then he nods, curt and quick.

"As long as you can swim!"
He dives into the broad canal
and lunges for the other bank.

I follow, and soon we're walking
southward down a broad avenue.
Construction workers swarm.

"A palace for the new emperor?"
I ask, but instead of answering,
he points to a sprawling market.

"The commercial plaza. Teeming
with nearly every item imaginable.
Performers, too. Come, Omaca!"

Tepaneca vendors recognize him,
regale us with tamales and sweets,
cloaks to keep off the growing chill.

I follow him toward the sound
of drums and flutes, near a statue
of Old Coyote, god of music and lust.

"Master Naltonac!" we shout, surprised,
at almost the same time. A traveling bard
famous back home and clearly here.

The man, hair streaked with white,
sings the final notes of a song
as a girl spins her dance to a stop.

"My daughter, Atotolin, friends!"
Cheers. Applause. Mecello pulls off
a bracelet he's just been given.

"Oh, singer," he requests,
setting the jewelry atop the drum.
"Give us the song of Tlacahuepan."

With a glance in my direction,
the bard grins and begins
a piece I've never heard—

The Mexica's patron god, Mextli,
Lord of Sun and War, had a friend
closer than any brother. Beloved.

To become chief of the pantheon,
the Lord of Sun and War
faced ancient divinities in battle.

By his side was Tlacahuepan,
fleet of foot, harbinger of death.
When the outcome seemed bleak—

Mextli's beloved rushed ahead
into a certain ambush, a sacrifice
that assured victory for his lord.

I notice Mecello's arm
pressing against mine
for the final lines . . .

The Death of Tlacahuepan

Naltonac, voice and drums. Atotolin, flute and dance.

A clamor of bells
out on the plains.
There, broken,
lies Tlacahuepan.

Mextli garlands him
with marigolds sweet
and sets him afire,
smoke curling aloft.

"Go not toward the vast
Unknowable Realm,
beloved of my heart.
Find a way back to me.

"The eagle will cry,
the jaguar will roar,
and like a fire-red swan,
you'll wheel through the skies."

They say only once
do we come to earth,
gods and humans,
a single chance.

But a love so great
can break all rules.
And Tlacahuepan
did indeed return.

Flying down from paradise
into his lover's arms again.

His Arms Around Me

Mecello

I have heard tell
of a certain bathhouse
attached to the temple
of Xochipilli, the god
who brings young men
together the way
I desperately yearn
to be with Omaca.

I tug at his cloak and
lead him in silence
past botanical gardens
to the shrine, festooned
with multihued flowers,
where a demure acolyte
leads us into a chamber
of steaming stone.

Other youths are present,
but I ignore those couples
as I take Omaca's face
in my hands, whispering,
"Is this okay with you?"

When he nods, I press
my greedy mouth to his,
and the cosmic wheels
seem to align at once,
as if the gods had planned
all along for this boy to put
his arms around me.

Aftermath

Omaca

Of course one of the Mexica pricks
reports our little trip to the priests.
They do some digging and find out
that we entered Xochipilli's shrine.

Another way the Mexica are weird—
everyone knows that lots of teens
have sex *in the calmecac itself,*
but the adults pretend not to notice.

In Tlaxcallan, we believe in openness.
There, I could just pick Mecello
as my boyfriend, no problem.
Except for the fact that he's a foreigner.

That last point is what makes Dad furious.
He and Mecello's father are called away
from their failing peace negotiations—
"Which have been further fraught and frayed,"
Dad growls, "by your willful disobedience."

Then he lets me have it—much worse
than a scolding or a beating—a decree
from the empress regent:
less than a fortnight of diplomacy left.

Then either an agreement will be reached
or the Flower Wars will resume.
No matter what, our time is done.
Mecello and I must part ways
in thirteen more days.

When Everyone's Asleep

Mecello

Thirteen days mean
thirteen nights, and
in the deepest dark
we find each other,
stifling moans and
cries in the hollows
of throat and shoulder.

Allies of the Heart

Omaca:
"The weird consequence—
bullies stay away from us
now that we're condemned."

Mecello:
"Ah, you foolish boy,
our love's an alliance—
we're stronger as one."

Our First Love Songs

Omaca:
I catch snatches of a song:
I glimpse him during spring,
walking by the light of dawn
along the bloom-dotted water.
He's like a sturdy chinampa
from which all flowers blossom.

As he strolls singing,
he is answered by lesser voices:
the racket-tailed motmots,
the blue grosbeaks,
the roseate spoonbills.
Listen in awe to my beloved,
Prince Mecello!

Mecello:
Harken closely! He twitters and trills
like some gorgeous demigod perched
in the branches of the Cosmic Tree.
The golden bells tied round his legs
are shaking out a rhythm like some
maraca-thrum hummingbird—
the very pounding of my heart!

Like fans of ruddy oriole plumes,
he opens wide his wings and soars
to the place where I await him,
breathless, beside flowery drums.
Behold my rare scarlet ibis—
Noble Omaca!

Farewells

Omaca

In a last-ditch effort, I rack my brain
for any crumb of gossip I've overheard
from the smug Mexica princes
or even Mecello himself,
and share it with my dad.

"Sadly, there is little in this information
that might change things.
Remember: That boy is your sworn enemy."

The empress regent takes the advice
of the warmongers on her council. The talks end.

We are back at a state of cold war.
Every fall, the Triple Alliance declares,
imperial troops will march their way
to the same battlefield near Chollolan,
and our forces must meet them there
to engage in another Flower War.

There's no escaping the inevitable—
even noble students in their final year
must leave their kingdom's calmecac
to prove their worth on scorched earth.

Avoiding battle deaths. Taking prisoners.
Dragging them back for ritual sacrifice.

Mecello and I say
our private goodbyes
in Xochipilli's bathhouse.
Tears and kisses and oaths.

To find each other again,
somehow, somewhere,
somewhen—
and together
make music that puts
the gods themselves
to shame.

The Bard in the Great Market of Tlatelolco

Mecello

Two months later, I accompany Mother
across the causeway between Mexico
and the eastern shore of Tepanecapan
to the sister city of Tenochtitlan—
Tlatelolco, home to the Great Market.

As she and her retinue search for fabric,
I wander toward Musicians' Alley
and hear a familiar baritone.

The bard Naltonac, accompanied as always
by his daughter, dancing flautist Atotolin.
His eyes go wide at the sight of me,
my jade-green cloak and jewelry.

"And now," he says, grinning at me,
"from Tizatlan, bright ruby of Tlaxcallan,
a new piece composed by Omaca,
son of their courageous general."

My heart nearly leaps from my chest
as he intones an achingly beautiful song
sent across hundreds of leagues,
a melodious message of love.

The final stanza echoes in my heart:

"I will see my dearest boy one day
where the maypole stands
festooned with blooms.
Like garlands we'll twist together
as heaven unravels its song."

The Bard in the Market of Chollolan

Omaca

For weeks I await Naltonac's return.
Word comes that he's performing nearby
in the busy market of our ally Chollolan.

I'm drunk with joy when he reveals that Prince Mecello,
too, has composed a beautiful love song to rival my own.

It begins with a flurry of beats:

"The drums are pounding in Tamoanchan!
The shield flowers spin round and round!
Ankle bells approach, with glittering ring!
Your timpani shimmers like blazing blooms
and shield flowers erupt in showers of sparks!

"Do I remember you? Ha! How could I forget?
You're my lover, the singer, the dancer.
But look how you've transformed yourself!
How did you manage this change, my boy?
You spread far and wide just like a song!

"You've become those sweet words themselves,
echoing warm and true wherever I go!"

Could Our Love Change Things?

Mecello

Back and forth
we fling melodies
and words through Naltonac.

In every lakeside town,
in every highland hamlet,
people have begun
to sing along.

By the fall,
everyone is talking
about the legendary love
between Prince Mecello
and his sworn enemy
Noble Omaca.

If we can embrace,
why can't they?

Why can't everyone?

The Flower War

Omaca

My father commands the army.
I'm now eighteen, a man
by our republic's standards.

I've got no choice but to strap on
the quilted armor, the shield,
the obsidian sword—and march.

It's unlike any real battle.
Both sides laid out in lines,
no deception, no strategy.

When the conch trumpet blows,
we rush each other, howling.

There's a collective grunt as we meet.

Then a chaos of movement,
striking and grappling, wrestling
opponents to the ground for capture.

For a while I struggle to take a prisoner,
but I stop and stand still when I see him,
jade helmet in the shape of a quetzal bird.

Seize Me

Mecello

I lower my sword, startled.
I was not prepared
to see him so arrayed—
a cape of scarlet feathers,
body painted black,
a ridge of hair atop his head.

An avatar of battle.
I could never stand
against such a man,
even if I didn't love him.

"Seize me," I mutter,
stepping close.
"It's the only way."

Nodding, he knocks
my blade aside
and pulls me down
to bind me tight.

Now, even if I die,
it will be by his hand,
gazing into those black eyes
that trapped my heart
and soul long ago.

My Choice

Omaca

Long ago I decided
that if this chance
ever came
I wouldn't hesitate.

I'm a citizen
of Tlaxcallan,
free to live as
I see fit.

To the Nine Hells
with honor, glory,
tradition, power.
All I want is him.

So as we march
from the field,
I lag behind
until those ahead
are rounding a hill.

Then I cut Mecello
loose and we run.

The Ocean

Mecello

Six months later,
Omaca and I sit on
a pebbly strand in
Huaxyacac, a coastal
kingdom untouched
by imperial expansion.

Hand in hand we watch as
the sun plunges iridescent
into waves at the edge
of the sea-ringed world.

Omaca turns to me, lovely face
glowing with that dying light.
"Priests say it spends the night
in the underworld, getting its fires
stoked by the Lord of Flame."

As twilight falls, I pull him close.
"So let us spend every night as well.
Let us be each other's sun."

His words are warm against my lips.
"And each other's Lord of Flame."

Rock Steady

By Charles Waters

For Traci Sorell, who always has my back

Morning Talk in Mirror

School is done, son!
Peace out, eighth grade.
Hello, summer,
it's nice to see you again!

Breakfast Talk

Too bad that feeling doesn't last.

Dad starts firing off words
before I have a chance to sit down
and attack these scrambled eggs.

"First off, after breakfast clean your room
like I asked yesterday.

"Secondly, your mother and I haven't gotten
over what you did last week.
You're treading on delicate ice.

"Third and last thing, Alonzo, from now on
your first, middle, and last name
is Work Work Work."

I wish my first, middle, and last name was

Leave Me Alone, Leave Me Alone, Leave Me Alone.
Of course, I keep that to myself.

Silver Lining

Hunched over in my room.
Staring at the walls as shadows
shift into different shapes.
I'm trying to look on the bright side.

My soul lifts like leaves in a gust of wind
when I think about how at least
I'll get to spend some time
with my best friend—who happens to be
fifty-six years older than me to the day.

Aggie Rae Moses

Grandma Aggie enjoys walking outside in bare feet.
"Alonzo, since I was a child in the country,
I've loved the feeling of earth under my soles."
She eats a tomato like an apple, one juicy chomp at a time,
sprinkles salt on it, "gives it an extra zip."
Grandma's one of a kind . . . and I like it.

How Grandma Sees Me

My report card was littered with Cs
for the eighth year in a row. At least I'm consistent.
"Do better," Dad said.
"Unacceptable." Mom said.
"You tried your best, baby." Grandma gave me a hug.

I struck out last spring with the bases loaded
to end the game, we were losing by one run.
"Keep your head down when you swing," Dad said.
"Stop looking so scared up there," Mom said.
"You're still my little big man." Grandma smiled.

When I headed up to get communion at church,
I tripped and wiped out on the burgundy carpet.
"Look down where you're walking," Dad said.
"Tie your shoelaces tighter," Mom said.
"You look so handsome in your new shirt."
Grandma straightened my collar.

She's my shield against the world.

Q-Ball and Tip-Top

My time used to be split between
Grandma and two brothers a year apart.
The Lockwood Boys of Blue Rock.

There's Quincy, whose nickname is Q-Ball
because he has a head shaped as if
someone's about to shoot pool with it.

And Tavares, whose nickname is Tip-Top
because he wants to be in tip-top shape at all times.
My dude wears ankle weights and hates junk food.

We called ourselves the Triumvirates.
They called me a "grandma's boy" because
sometimes when they'd ask if I wanted
to go hang with them, I'd say,
"Not today. I'm hanging out with Ms. Aggie Rae."

They'd shake their heads, whisper, "Cornball."

I'd laugh, pretend that word didn't bother me
while knots twisted in my stomach.

When we'd get together, me, Q-Ball, and Tip-Top
made videos on our phones, played basketball, rode our bikes,
had sleepovers. We were tight, until last week.

Summertime Decision

It was after school, seven more days before vacation.

I was looking for Q-Ball and Tip-Top
so we could walk home together.
I found them near the Frederick Douglass statue,
heads down, streams of smoke flowing out
their mouths, each of them passing along a vape.

I could not believe it.

They were with Miquan, Freddie, and Xavier,
three of the most popular kids in school.
They were vaping, too.

There was so much smoke it looked as if
everybody had gotten swallowed by an afternoon fog.

In this mist, Q-Ball and Tip-Top waved me over.
I hesitated, then shuffled toward them.
"What are you doing?" I asked. "Chill, man,"
Q-Ball whispered. I muttered to Tip-Top, "Dude,
all you care about is being healthy. I don't get it."
He chuckled, "Try it? It's not so bad." I looked at
Q-Ball, who said, "Go ahead, man."

He handed me his vape pen.

It felt as if the world had closed in around me.
I might as well have been a vape-holding statue called Scared.
Q-Ball and Tip-Top shook their heads, looked down,
whispered, "Cornball." I hate that word.
A knot gripped my stomach again.

I know I should've walked away; I know what I was
thinking was wrong as the night is long and still . . .
Eff it, I thought. "Why not?" I took a puff,
sputtered out some smoke before coughing so hard
I thought my lungs would slingshot out of my mouth.

Everyone laughed, except me.

Freddie slowly closed his eyes. "Idiot."
Miquan waved him off. "Leave him alone."
Xavier stared at his Jordans. "You should go."
Q-Ball's and Tip-Top's eyes burned into mine.
"Go hang out with your grandma!"
No one laughed, which surprised me. Instead
their eyes went wide as a full moon.

When I turned around to see what was up,
there was our principal, Mrs. Kubrick, staring
at me, the vape pen still clutched in
my fingers.

The Disbelieved

That night Mom and Dad took turns yelling
at me so loud I thought I'd lose my hearing.
I've never heard my full name,
Alonzo Nathaniel Moses, said so many times.

My punishment read like a schedule written in
big bold letters by the haters of all haters:
**Home, school, home, chores, school, home,
chores, school** for the rest of the week.
After that, a summer job.

Q-Ball and Tip-Top threw me so far under the bus
I'm now a permanent part of its braking system.
Both said they were walking by, saw me vaping, and
were telling me to stop when Mrs. Kubrick showed up.
Freddie, Miquan, and Xavier said the same thing.
She believed them.

So did Mom and Dad.
That's what hurt so much.
More than the punishment.
How could they not believe me?
Their own flesh and blood.
Their own son?

As they were taking turns yelling at me,
I remember counting my breaths, in and out,
in and out, trying to keep it steady.
Rock steady. Staring ahead. Hands folded.
Tuning out my parents' voices.

Every time I said "They're lying, that's not true" and tried
to explain what really happened, they shook their heads.
"Stop interrupting us."

I See You

Grandma stood in the other room behind Mom and Dad.
They didn't notice, but I did.

She was slowly raising her hands up and down
like a conductor
to get my breaths to match hers.

Dinner

Birds chirping their evening song.
Cars passing by once in a while.
Cups being picked up and put down.
Forks gently scraping against the plates.
No sounds of anyone talking.

Explanation

You could have cut the tension in our house
with a buzz saw for real for real.
I was hunched over in my room,
hands on my head, listening to music
when Grandma knocked on the door five times—
how I always knew it was her.

She sat down across from me. Touched my hand.
"Do you want to tell me what happened?"
I swallowed hard, my eyes brimming with tears.

"Okay."

I spilled everything out, fast as a waterfall;
she put her hands in prayer, fingers pressed
against her lips, and said, "Mm-hmm, mm-hmm."

When I stopped talking, she smoothed out
her jogging suit. "Well, you were wrong
to smoke—you know it, I know it, so do your parents."

The air was still.

Our eyes met.

"I never smoked before and I never will again," I finally said.
"I'm sorry for messing up."

Her face was unreadable.

"Do you believe me?"

She leaned forward, wiped the tears from
my eyes, broke into a warm grin.
"I believe you."

Eavesdropping

Bodies are weird.

I had barely looked at my dinner
with Mom and Dad thinking I was a liar.
After Grandma said she believed me,
I could have eaten a building.

I went to the kitchen to do some work
on a turkey sandwich when I heard
voices in the living room. I tiptoed, quiet as a cat,
through the hallway.

Mom, Dad, and Grandma were talking.
Like scattered puzzle pieces I was able
to put together what was being said.

Can't this wait till tomorrow, Mom?

No, son, it can't.
You both ride that boy about every little thing.
His grades, sports, finding a job.
I guarantee you're going to ruin his spirit.

Aggie Rae, you're my mother-in-law and I love and respect you dearly, but you know good and well it's not your place to tell us how to raise Alonzo.

Tammi's right, Mom. Look, Dad was hard on me
and I turned out okay.

Lorenz, you and your father never got on solid
footing BECAUSE he was so hard on you.
You're as stubborn as him, too.

Don't go there. You've been bringing
this up about me and Dad for years.

Why don't you both believe him about this
smoking vape whatchamacallit?
You didn't raise a liar.

He lied about forging our signatures on a test he took, Aggie Rae.

That was two years ago!

Quincy and Tavares are good kids, Mom.

So is your son!

My mind twirled like a hurricane
as I tiptoed back to my room.

I wasn't hungry anymore.

Good Riddance

I haven't talked to Q-Ball and Tip-Top
since the vaping thing
and I don't know if I ever will.
They've been taking up way
too much space in my brain.

What a bunch of punks.

Shiloh and Winston

Before the Triumvirates formed, I also hung out
with two other people, our very own mini Justice League:

Shiloh, who lives next door, wears her hair in different
braided hairstyles, and has a smile so warm it could
melt an iceberg.

And Winston, who lives down the street, is thin
as a beanstalk, wears braces, and would give a stranger
his jacket if they were cold.

All five of us have known each other since preschool.

We helped blow out candles at birthday parties,
played together in the park—where Shiloh would school all
of us in basketball—and had a group chat where we talked
about anime, favorite NBA teams, and why homework sucks.

Things changed, slow as syrup at first: Winston transferred to
a private school, then stuff picked up faster than the Flash
when Q-Ball and Tip-Top started crushing on Shiloh,
and then we caught Shiloh and Winston making out in the park

with so much energy I thought their faces would come off.
For almost two years I stayed friends with both groups.
Grandma said I was a teenage Switzerland, neutral to both sides.

Game Show Heaven

Now that I'm on summer "vacation"
I spend every day looking for a job.
My hand is about to fall off from
filling out so many applications.

When I get home, Grandma is watching
her favorite game show, *Pyramid*.
An airline pilot is in the Winner's Circle.
This means he could win $100,000 if the other
person, some TV actor, helps him guess
the correct answers in sixty seconds or less.
With five seconds to go
there's one more question. "Hurry up!"
Grandma yells again just as the airline pilot
guesses correctly and wins.
"Yes!" Grandma cheers, pumping her fist,
smiling brighter than starshine.

That woman loves two things:
her family and rooting for people.

Commercial Break

Grandma and I are watching commercials,
sipping lemonade. I feel a knot twisted up in
my stomach again.
"What's wrong?" she asks.

I stare at the stuccoed ceiling,
feeling like I'm looking at upside-down ocean waves.
Makes sense, my life's upside down.

I take a deep breath, catching the scent of Grandma's
cocoa butter lotion before exhaling.
"You know, last week I heard you talking
to Mom and Dad about them not believing me."

She stares ahead, takes a deep breath,
then shifts her body, eyes now focused on mine.
"So, what did you think?"
I feel frustration rising up in my throat.
"Nothing I do is ever good enough for them. I'm so sick of it.
Sick of it." I smack the cushion, *thwat!*
Sounds like a fastball hitting the catcher's mitt.

She grabs my hand—hers is smaller than I remember,
and cold as ice, which helps cool off my temper.
"Alonzo, people are complicated. It's the way God built us.
They love you very much even if they show it in funny ways."

Press Your Luck

Another game show is on, this one called *Press Your Luck*.
Grandma loves this stuff more than flowers
love sunshine and rain. We stay silent until
I decide to press my own luck and ask something
I've been wondering about for a long time.

"Why do Mom and Dad hate me?"

Grandma turns, stares into my soul,
her eyes beginning to water.

My face heats up. I look down at the hardwood floor,
embarrassed. Only sounds are the audience on TV
cheering for some contestant who won a trip to Puerto Vallarta.

Wish I could go there now and take back what I asked.

The longer we sit, the more I want to jump out of my skin.
I don't know what to say or do.

Finally, Grandma pierces the silence.
"Alonzo, they don't hate you. They're passing down how they
were treated as kids."

She takes a sip of ice tea, plays with her silver bracelets—
that's how I can tell she's super nervous—then says,
"Your mom's parents were traveling missionaries, discipline
was all she knew until she moved back to the states
and met your father in college.

"Your grandpa Nathaniel mellowed out when you knew him.
Before that, though, I used to call him Sergeant because
he bossed around your father too much. I got on him
for years to chill out until there was an argument so bad
your dad stopped speaking to him.

"About broke me in half seeing my family splintered.

"When we got a call that your mother was pregnant, that's
when things cooled out between him and your father.
It was an uneasy truce. Ridiculous it took all that for my
husband to wake up, not be such a pain in the you know where."

My brain is on overload. "Why didn't anybody ever tell me this
before?" I ask.

"Too painful," she said, turning off the TV.

Feels as if my life has always been sort of like a wrinkled shirt
and now things are slowly starting to get ironed out a little bit.

Work

Filling out all those applications was worth it.
I've got a summer job! Only took a week to get one.
At Maisy's Ice Cream Shoppe
I serve up sweet treats, sweep floors,
clean tables and bathrooms, take out
the trash, then sleep like an infant when I get home.

Shiloh and Winston work there too.
Since they started going out last year,
I can count how many days we've spent together on one hand.
I'd see Shiloh at school, but it was a quick hi and bye
because she has her own friends now.
She's trying to play Cupid and hook me up with one of them.

Her name is Tori Hendrix.
Family moved to Blue Rock from a town
called Apple Blossom last year. She has pink braces,
kind eyes, and wears patent leather sneakers.

In early spring I tripped going up the stairs
at school on the second-floor landing.
Total wipeout, arms and legs all over the place
like an octopus.

Embarrassed doesn't even describe it, I wanted
to snap my fingers and disappear so bad.
A monsoon of laughter and pointing.
The only one who didn't laugh or point,

the only one who helped me up,
the only one who helped me tamp down my shame
was Tori.

I do like her; she seems so out of my league, though. She gets straight As, is the best athlete at school, and smells like fresh laundry.

"You two would go together like PB and J," Shiloh says.
OMG.

My heart starts dancing faster than a butterfly on a sugar rush.

I try talking, but all that comes out is "Uh, uh, well,
I don't know, it's just that, uh, it's just, uh, well,
I don't know."

Shiloh smiles, rubs my arm. "It's okay. Breathe.
Never mind. It's all good."

Something Wicked

In English class last year, we studied Shakespeare.
My mind sometimes felt like it was getting hit with a stick
with all those weird words.
One thing I did understand was this couplet:
By the pricking of my thumbs,
Something wicked this way comes.

At the start of summer
Grandma's wicked thing started off slow at first,
an occasional cough here and there,
almost like a tease. I didn't really notice it
except when looking back.

Now, two weeks later, it's become
as constant as the days of the week.
Body jerks so hard from coughing,
you would think Satan himself
has gotten ahold of her.

Finally, the unspoken becomes spoken.

Words fire off back and forth like a tennis match.

"You have to go."
"No, I don't."
"You have to go."
"No, I won't."
"You have to go."
"Why?"
"Because we said so."
"No, no, no, no, no."

I pray for at least a pocket of sun to spread
some light into this darkness.

Finally, at six a.m., Grandma agrees to go to the hospital.

All the Smoke

Grandma had smoked cigarettes since she was thirteen.
"That's what people did back then," she'd say to me.
Grandpa Nathaniel died from them when I was five.
I barely remember him except his cheeks felt like sandpaper
when I kissed them and he used a cologne called Brut 33.

When he passed on, Grandma wore nicotine patches,
chewed nicotine gum, went under hypnosis,
anything to quit, which she finally did.

Despite all this she never lost what she calls
her "sunny disposition."

Mom and Me

Dad calls, says they're running tests.
At breakfast Mom picks at her raisin bagel.
"You don't have to go to the ice cream shop today."
I spoon my cereal up, then turn it sideways
so it drops like a sugary waterfall.
"It's okay. I need to do something."
She nods, taps her bagel against the plate.
"I need to water your grandmother's azaleas."

Concern

Work goes by in a daze.

Hours melt away.

The only words I've said are
"Welcome" and "Thank you for stopping by."
Shiloh and Winston occasionally stare at me.
Since Shiloh's mom, Dr. Martin, is picking us up,
like usual, I have no choice but to wait with them after work.
"The first month of summer has flown by," Winston says.
I don't say anything. Far as I'm concerned, I already want to kick
the rest of summer to another dimension, galaxy, solar system.
"What's wrong?" Shiloh asks.
"You've been quiet since this morning."
I try to talk, nothing comes out. I hunch my shoulders.
"Well," Winston says, "you have both our cells.
We're always here if you need us."

I nod. I appreciate the offer, but right now,
I'm not up for talking to anyone except family.

Family Meeting

The four of us sit on our covered deck.
At least the sunset's in a good mood.
Streaks of orange paint the sky.

My arms are folded as if that will block
bad news.

Dad opens his mouth, nothing comes out.

Mom tries, same thing.

Finally, Grandma says, "Alonzo, I have cancer.
I have an appointment tomorrow to start my treatment."
My folded arms can't stop tears leaking from my eyes.
Or loosen the knot forming in my stomach again.

Mom and Dad rub my back.
Grandma whispers in my ear,
"I'm going to be fine."

How can she be so sure?

Feeling the Love

Word spreads
faster than an eyeblink about Grandma
because she's the one doing the spreading.
She posted about it online.
"You know our town," she said.

"Folks are going to find out anyway,
might as well control the narrative."
The likes and comments
burst through the stratosphere.
Donations made to the American
Cancer Society in her honor.
Homemade dinners dropped off at our house.
Grandma even got back in touch
with long-lost childhood friends.
Rays of daylight slicing through a dark time.

Being There

Grandma's shadow doesn't follow
her as closely as we do.

She wants tea?
I sprint to the kitchen to make it.

She needs an extra pillow?
Dad gets one faster than a lightning strike.

She asks for a back rub,
Mom's soft fingers are ready to go.

Grandma smiles, says, "You all know
how to make an old lady feel special."

You better effin' believe it.

Because of Cigarettes

I usually say the same thing this time of year,
you could set your watch by it:

July is too dang hot!
I'm a walking puddle of sweat!
We might as well live on top of the sun!

Right now, though, I'd take July weather every day
if it would make my best friend feel better.
Grandma coughs more;
"hacking" is what she calls it.
It happens watching game shows,
reading her mystery books,
working in her garden.

Grandma has shortness of breath;
"sucking wind" is what she calls it.
It happens walking short distances,
standing too long, taking a nap.

Grandma now spits up blood;
"spewing out plasma" is what she calls it.
It happens talking on the phone,
getting her weekly mani-pedi,
wrapping a scarf around her head.
She whispers, "Those damn cigarettes."

Changes

Sometimes, after dinner, there's food
left on my plate, especially vegetables.

Sometimes there are clothes
on my bedroom floor.

Sometimes books and papers
are scattered on my desk.

All of this would usually lead to
Mom and Dad being jerks to me.

But lately, it's been different.

Dad brought out some lemonade
after I mowed the lawn, then said,
"Excellent work."

Mom hugged me after I ironed her clothes
because she had been too tired from work to do it.
"Thank you, sweetie," she said.

I appreciate the effort, but I keep wondering:
Why does it take someone getting sick
for them to be nice to me?

Why can't our family communicate
and understand each other better?
It feels as if—to quote Grandma—
there's an "uneasy truce."

How can I break the family chain?

Distraction

Watching Grandma sleep on the couch
makes me calm and nervous at the same time.
She's been telling me for weeks,
"Baby, I don't have much energy."
I focus on her slow, rhythmical breathing
when my cell buzzes. It's Shiloh.
Gokart racing w me and Winston today?
I ask Dad, who says, "Yes, it'll be good to clear your
mind a little." I text Shiloh back, u got it!

The Blue Rock 500

Zipping by in my electric kart,
the Alonzo competitive spirit in full effect.

As the lead changes, we keep shouting out
Black race car drivers past and present.

I pass Shiloh and Winston around the bend.
"Bubba Wallace!"

When we get to the next level of the track,
Shiloh flies past me and Winston.
"Cheryl Linn Glass!"

Heading toward the highest level,
Winston slips by both of us.
"Lewis Hamilton!"

Hitting the straightaway toward the final stretch:
We're neck and neck and neck.
Our karts could whisper to each other they're so close.

"I'm going to win!"
"This is mine!"
"I'm the champ!"

When we zip past the finish line,
one thing becomes clear:
For the sake of us not starting World War III—

we call it a tie.

I didn't think about Grandma the whole time.
Weird. Don't know if that's a good thing or not?

Driving Home

When Dr. Martin picks us all up,
my body feels reenergized, like I've been baptized.
We have boxes with leftover pizza and smiles
temporarily tattooed on our faces

until we spot Q-Ball, Tip-Top, Miquan,
Freddie, and Xavier outside the arcade, vaping.

Dr. Martin's head turns so fast
I thought she might get whiplash.
"You've got to be kidding me."
She hits the brakes, gets out of the car,
marches toward them barking out
orders like a football coach.
"Quincy and Tavares Lockwood, get over here!
I'm calling your mother right now."

Their faces are frozen in fear.

They look like vape-holding statues
called *I Done Effed Up*.
It's going to be a loooong night for them.

Vindication is mine!

Friday-Night Healing

When I get back, Grandma's on the couch
watching Game Show Network. They're having
a marathon of *Pyramid*.
The TV is on mute, though.

Mom and Dad are beside her.
"Would you have a seat?" Dad says.

I sit across from them.

Both their faces look as if they've been dropped
in a desert without a map.

Lost.

Dad scratches the back of his head.
He does that when he's super nervous.

"Mrs. Lockwood called."

Mom smooths out the edges around her temples.
She does that when she's super nervous.

"Quincy and Tavares will stop by to apologize tomorrow."

I stare at the family portrait taken when I was in preschool.
Grandma, Grandpa, Mom, Dad, and me.
Our smiles wider than the Pacific Ocean.
For weeks and weeks, I'd been too worried about
Grandma's cancer to really care about any of this.
But now?
My insides feel like a volcano about to erupt.

"We're sorry for not believing you," they whisper.

My face flushes.
They should have trusted me from the jump. For real for real.
I try to press down these feelings.

"It's just that . . ."

Words rush from my mouth, hot as lava.

"No!" I yell. "Stop trying to make excuses,
you should have believed me!"

Grandma smiles so small an ant might not see it.
Mom's mouth drops like an anvil; Dad's eyebrows rise.

"I tried telling you the truth about what happened
but you wouldn't listen.
Before Grandma got sick, you treated me like I couldn't do
anything right. You need to start believing in me!"

I've never talked to my parents like this.

Mom and Dad look at Grandma, look at each other, then
look at me.

I lean back, feeling as if a mountain has been
lifted off my spirit.

If they put me on punishment for yelling at them, fine.
I said what I said, and I meant every word of it.

Possibilities

I'm whipping up breakfast for Grandma and me:
tofu scramble sprinkled with turmeric,
a small bowl of fresh fruit, and a cup of herbal tea.

It's as if someone took an Etch A Sketch and shook
my life clean, so now I have a fresh start.

Grandma shuffles in, sits down, then claps her hands
as I put the tray in front of her.

"It smells so good. Look at you, making breakfast
for your bestie. My baby is so talented."

I roll my eyes. "Bestie? Will you stop talking
like you're my age."

"I feel your age. I don't feel mine.
I've never looked at myself as old."

We sit in silence.
In our house, silences are usually as itchy
as a new sweater; today, though, it feels
more comforting than a cup of hot chocolate
in winter.

"Way to speak truth to power last night, kiddo.
I do think you played your one and only
'yelling at your parents and getting away with it' card."

I laugh so hard the herbal tea I was drinking rushes out
of my nose.

"Alonzo, been thinking a lot about your grandfather lately and
about how life can be an open road with endless possibilities.

"I'm grateful for the road I took with my life.

"You know your grandfather almost didn't ask me out on a date.

"He was scared to even talk to me.
Said girls made his stomach somersault.

"There was another boy who was sweet on me as well;
he didn't have your grandfather's dark, striking eyes, and those
two dimples on his cheeks, either.

"In our day boys asked girls out and not the other way around.
Besides, if I had asked him out first, he might have passed out.
Glad he did ask, though; if he hadn't, you wouldn't be here."

My outer voice says, "Glad he asked you out, too."
My inner voice says, "Is Grandma a mind reader?"

Taking Chances

The bell above the door rings as I walk into work,
one foot in front of the other.
Breathe, dude, breathe. My legs feel like jelly,
heart beating faster than an express train.
I'm sweating so much from nerves you'd have
thought I just got out of the ocean.

There's only Shiloh and Winston and me inside
the store since it doesn't open for a half hour and our
manager is in his office.

You can do this; you can do this!

Winston asks, "Dude, what's wrong?"
Shiloh says, "Are you okay?"

Speak, Alonzo, speak!
"Let's hang out tomorrow at the arcade.
Maybe you could ask Tori to join us?"

Their eyes about pop out of their faces.

"Yes and yes! I'm so happy! Tori has been crushing on you
for months. I almost gave up hope."

"Hell yeah, brother, that's what I'm talking about!
That's what I'm talking a-bout!"

"Good," I say, then power walk to the break room
because I'm blushing so bright, I probably look like a tomato.

Rock Steady

Summer vacation feels like a boulder going downhill:
It picks up speed as it goes.

Hard to believe we're in mid-August.

School starts next week. I go shopping
for new clothes with Mom; I use some of
the money from my job to buy them.
"Way to be independent, Alonzo," she says.
"Your father's proud of you, too."

We're not talking about the main thing.

Grandma has an appointment tomorrow to check on her tumor.

When we get home, she's sitting on the couch
knitting a sky-blue sweater.
Man, she's lost a lot of weight. Her hip bones poke out
of her flowered dress like a pair of scissors.
"Come here, sit next to an old lady who's young at heart,"
she says, waving me over.

I plop down.

"This sweater's for you. Fall will be here
before you know it." We stare at the TV.
"You know, life is not a sure thing.

No one's going to live forever.
A body has only so much mileage in it.
Life is about savoring every moment because
one never knows when it will go away."

I close my eyes, take a deep breath.
"You're going to be fine."
She keeps looking at the TV while gently
resting her hand on mine. I swallow hard.
"You're such a good kid," she whispers.
"Such a good kid."

I whisper back,
"I learned from the best."

The Water Clock

BY PADMA VENKATRAMAN

India, twelfth century

My First Love

I'm five
the first time
I fall in love.

Appa's still working hard, I see, because his oil lamps
are burning brightly.
I know it's past my bedtime, but I creep
into Appa's study and skulk
in the shadows cast by the flickering
yellow flames.

"Shouldn't you be asleep?"
He sounds more amused than annoyed, so I
climb onto his wide, warm lap and stretch
a curious finger out
toward the palm-leaf manuscript
he's poring over.

Tracing the numbers and letters
he's been etching into the long, dry leaves, I ask,
"What are you writing about?"

His soft, bright eyes
gaze at his palm-leaf manuscript
the way he often looks at Amma.

"Magic," he breathes.

Magic? What fun!
"I want to learn!"

Appa leads me
to the open courtyard
in the center of our home.
He places a twig in my palm.
Silvered by moonlight, the twig
looks as shiny as a new writing nail.
His large fingers guide mine and we
write in the dirt together:
0 1 2 3 4 5 6 7 8 9.

"This is not magic!"
I stomp my feet.

"Leela, numbers are where the magic
of mathematics begins,
although not where it ends.
Students and scholars from all over the world
swarm to Ujjayani University as bees to nectar
thirsting to study mathematics
because it speaks a universal tongue
people everywhere understand."

He presses my palm on his chest.
I feel his lifeblood
drumming. One, two. One, two.

"Numbers are the heartbeat of our universe.
With numbers we remember
time, as Bhumadevi circles Surya."

"But—doesn't the sun circle our Earth?" I exclaim.

He replies, "Some scholars think so, but I don't.
According to the astronomer Aryabhatta,
who numbered the steps of heavenly dancers,
it's Mother Earth who circles the Sun God.
I believe Aryabhatta is right because he trusts mathematics.
Mathematics is Goddess Saraswathi's music.
Mathematics reflects the magnificence of creation."

Appa's words are a poem.
An intriguing invitation.
I don't understand them with my mind. But
I feel them ringing in my heart.

Patterns

I'm six when Amma decides to teach me
and my cousin Maheshvari
how to create a kolam.

We grab fistfuls of fine powder and draw
blobs.

We're impatient, but Amma says, "Keep trying
and one day, your lines
will go where you want."

She makes a grid with dots. 1, 1, 2, 3, 5 . . .
Patterns blossom on the floor as she draws
lines through her dots,
creating diamonds and stars,
circles and flowers.

I make my own grid.
1, 1, 2, 3, 5 . . .

Looking down at me, Appa asks,
"Guess what number comes next?"

In my mind, dots come alive.
If there's an invisible zero in front of the first . . .
0, 1, 1, 2, 3, 5, then what?
I know!
Each new number's the sum
of the two that came before.
"Eight, thirteen, twenty-one!"

Appa smiles. "Perhaps we should have named her Hema.
For Hemachandra, who described
this sequence most elegantly in his study of poetry."

Amma argues, "Not more elegantly
than the women of his family.
We women described it with kolam art
centuries before he was born, surely."

The proud tilt of Amma's head
shows me two things:

1. Her argument has beaten his.
2. Women can be better mathematicians than men.

When Appa Teaches Me Mathematics

Numbers
hold my hands and I
hold numbers in my heart,
faithful to mathematics
alone
until I fall in love

a second time
at seventeen.

From Afar

He's a blurred line of movement,
catching the corner of an eye
as I turn away from the dawn sky and look
down across the still grounds
of Ujjayani University, from the high tower
where I've been aiding Appa with his observations.

Appa's echoing footsteps
descend the winding stairs
but I linger, staring
at the stranger's lithe figure
as intently, as curiously,
as I watch the heavens.

Silhouetted against a bright flicker of sunlight,
his head is clean-shaven, smooth as a monk's.
His movements are also smooth—but a soldier's,
not a dancer's. Powerful—yet graceful.
His movements remind me of our martial art form,
which my little brother, Lokasamudra, wants to learn.

"Leela?" Appa calls. I hurry after him.
As I emerge from the shadow of the tower,
stripes of sunlight yellow the earth.

I see the young man clearly. Oblivious to us,
he continues exercising. Crouching, leaping,
kicking out, punching an invisible adversary.

He twists. His shirt is open at the neck, offering me
a glimpse of his long, rippling muscles,
his beautifully sculpted face.
His focused eyes
aren't
distracted by us.

"That's Xiang," Appa says. "A visiting scholar from China.
Young. Yet wise. Mind as brilliant as a diamond.
As for what he's doing, it's one of their martial-art forms,
not unlike our kalaripayittu."

"Beautiful," I murmur.

"Indeed." Appa glances
up at the gilded clouds.
"A spectacular sunrise."

Appa doesn't understand that for once,
I've found an earthly object
more fascinating than any heavenly one.

Brothers and Secrets

"You don't look tired at all!"
Lokasamudra exclaims when we return.
"Your eyes are all sparkly.
Did a new star sprout
in the heavens or something?"

"Don't be silly," I reply in my bossiest
elder-sister voice.
"Stars don't sprout."

Flower

"Jasmine? Or marigold?" My cousin Maheshvari
lifts two strings of flowers.

"Whichever you prefer."

"What's wrong?" She cocks her head. "A week ago
you were more excited than me
to see Kalidasa's new play!"

I shrug. "You enjoy dressing up more than I do."
She can't argue with that.

Maheshvari always played mother to her dolls,
dressing and cuddling them, singing them to sleep.
I played teacher instead,
lecturing my dolls on astronomy and arithmetic,
repeating each lesson Appa taught me.

Only a few hours younger than I, Maheshvari is more sister
than cousin. Our families live under the same roof,
ruled by our grandfather.
"You choose whatever flowers you want to wear.
I don't care. I'll take what's left," I tell her.

"Fine. Then you get jasmine
because it looks like the stars you love so much."
She yanks my hair as she braids it with flowers.
It hurts, as usual, but I'm unusually silent,
wondering   where Xiang spends his evenings and how,
wondering   where he is now,
wondering   if I'll ever see him again.

Probably not.
I'm fated to be unlucky.

Mind at Play

My fate must be changing!
He's come to see the play, too!
Seated in a place of honor, as we are.
Seated in our row!

I never thought any man's profile
could interest me more than a play by Ujjayani's
most masterful writer.

Introduction

After the play ends, Xiang walks over!
Presses his palms together and bows his head.

Appa, Lokasamudra, and Maheshvari echo his greeting.
I try to control the excitement
bubbling inside me.

"My niece, Maheshvari," Appa says. "My son, Lokasamudra,
and my daughter, Leelavathi, of whom I spoke to you."

Xiang's eyes widen in surprise.
"Surely, lady, it is not you
who helped the acharya test the chakravala method
of solving indeterminate equations?"

Handsome, attractive, an almost perfect accent, but
unfortunately, just as bigoted as most men.

My excitement cools
like a pot of boiling rice pulled off a hot stove. "Why
should it not be me, sir?"

A smile twitches on Appa's lips.

"Forgive me, lady." Xiang's voice is soft, sincere, musical.
"When your father mentioned your mathematical prowess,
my mind conjured up an image of an older woman.
Wisdom in one so young
is rare, if I may be permitted to say so."

I've been gawked at before by boys.
I've seen men stare at me as if
I were a toy they wished they could play with.

Xiang gazes at me as if he's seeing a goddess.
With admiration and respect bordering on reverence.

I've never been more thankful
Maheshvari insisted I dress up.

Backdrop

"How appropriate that today's play was about love!"
Maheshvari teases as soon as we're alone.
"He's beautiful, brilliant, and not at all my type,"
she continues. "If he were to write a love letter,
he'd surely compose it with numbers, not words."

Nothing wrong with that.

Next Day

"Xiang has asked for your help
with his translations," Appa says.
"I assume you are willing?"

My heart flutters
like a leaf lifted by a cool breeze.

"Leela can't spend time unchaperoned
with a young man!" my grandfather objects.

"They won't be alone! In the library, they will be surrounded
by scribes, students, and scholars!" Appa reassures him. "But
we can also ask Lokasamudra to accompany them.
I'm honored by Xiang's request and so I *will* honor it."

My grandfather mutters but says no more.

I know why he let it go.

From Birth I Was Cursed by the Unluckiest Star

My horoscope predicts
my husband will die
within a year of marriage.

Being born
under an
unlucky star never bothered me
until now.

Unmarriageable, I was
allowed
to chart the steps of star dances
to study the songs numbers sing.
Now I may be falling in love
allowed or not . . .

But I can never marry.

How could I ever risk
anyone dying for the love of me
especially—dare I even think of this—
someone as brilliant as Xiang?

But he's safe. Surely he doesn't
love me?

And Yet

I astonish myself and Maheshvari
by lining my eyes with kajal
before Lokasamudra and I leave for the library.

I spot Xiang reading by the window,
his perfectly chiseled face scowling
with concentration, sunlight shining
on his bare scalp.

Lokasamudra lets the door creak shut.
He seeks out a faraway corner, sets up a chessboard,
and starts moving the pieces, playing by himself.

Xiang's glowing eyes meet mine.
"A joy to see you, lady.
Thank you for helping me translate more accurately."

"So much gratitude already, sir?
We haven't begun yet." I smile.

Scribes and students stare at us, but we
waste no more time. I discover in Xiang
my most intense, intelligent student,
my most cheerful, easygoing colleague.

Our conversation soon flows
away from mathematics.
Our voices rise and grow
as we share stories and laugh
together until the gong reminds us
we have run out of time.

In My Nature

The more we work together,
the more wretched and elated I feel.

Surely our fingers touch more
often than strictly accidentally?
Surely we sit closer together
than my grandfather would like?

I should protect my heart.
I should invent an excuse
never to meet Xiang again.
Yet I cannot.

Brahmagupta says bodies fall to Earth
because it is in Earth's nature to attract
just as it is in water's nature to flow.

Xiang attracts me like Earth.

It is not in my nature to stop
falling
closer,
steeper,
deeper
in love.

Faint Hope

Even as I silently promise myself I
shall never endanger Xiang by marrying him,
I remind myself there is a dim ray of hope.

For as long as I can remember, Appa's been searching
for a solution to counter my horrible horoscope prediction.
He's asked his friend, the best astrologer in the land,
to find out if someday there may be
a favorable conjunction of planets and stars
that would annul my bad luck and provide
a window of time
during which I might actually
marry a man without bringing him harm.

I pray an answer will suddenly blaze in the astrologer's mind
shedding unassailable light on a way out of my dilemma.
Soon. Somehow.
Before Xiang finishes his studies and leaves Ujjayani.

Calculating Predictions

Xiang doubts some of the sentences he translates.
He disputes some accepted theories that scholars
have taken for granted since
before the first Gupta monarch took the throne.

Xiang says to calculate is to create music with truth,
but he abhors trying to predict the future. He says
horoscopes are lies—at best innocuous, at worst horrible.

Aghast, I ask, "Don't you believe our lives are foretold
by the positions of the stars?"

He challenges, “If so, then shouldn’t Chinese astrology work
exactly like your system?
The rules of astronomy are governed by mathematics.
So they are the same everywhere. They are the truth.
Astrology is nothing but a lie.”

“You can’t know that,”
I argue.

“I can.” His jaw tightens. He takes a heavy breath.
“Astrologers predicted a phenomenal future
for both me and my beloved twin brother
when we were born. Long, prosperous lives.
He died of smallpox, five years ago.
I survived without a single scar
although my stars
were no different than his.”

My hand reaches out to his before I can stop it.
Our fingers weave together before I force myself to pull away.
My fist clenches as if it wants
to hold the warmth
of our shared touch forever.

Confused

Once, I look up and see Xiang’s eyes are fixed
on me, rather than on the manuscript
we’re supposed to be studying.
I don’t want to turn away.
He doesn’t seem to, either.
I’m sure we’ll smile away the hour.
But then I see a glint of sadness in his eyes.
And he turns away from me.

He's a human puzzle who is harder to understand
than any mathematical conundrum I've met.
If only my heart could solve problems as easily as my mind!
Sometimes I'm sure there's more than mere admiration
in his gaze. Then I'm sure he's holding a part of his soul
back from me, and I'm reading too deeply into gestures
that only affirm friendship.

Sharing My Secret

"What's wrong?" my mother asks. "You seem so
preoccupied these days. Is that Chinese scholar
working you too hard?"

"No! I just—I just wish I had a life outside the library."
Tears prick the back of my eyes, and I try to keep them there.

"You want to have your own family, your own
loving home, too?" My mother guesses correctly.
"There's no shame in that, Leela."

"But there's no point wishing for the impossible."

"It's not impossible. I wasn't sure whether to share this,
but . . . you know your father has always sought
to see if there might be a conjunction of planets
that would annul the bad luck foretold at the time of your birth.
He has met a brilliant new astrologer
who specializes in cases like yours. I am praying and hoping
this astrologer and your father, working together,
will soon find a way for you to love
more than just mathematics. I am sure they will succeed."

That night, I dare to let my soul
wander further in my dreams than ever before.

Almost Complete

Xiang works   too quickly,
racing through
his translation   too soon.

"When you're finished with this tome,
will you translate another?"
I voice my desperate hope.

"When I am done,
I must prepare
for my journey home."

Two Pieces

It's better this way,
one half of me says.

Better he move far away
than live nearby and marry another.
Or worse,
marry me, then
die months later.

The other half of me
cries. Why?

Isn't a short life
filled with love
better than an
        unfulfilled eternity?

Good News

"Leela?" Lokasamudra, little though he is,
senses something is wrong as we walk home.
"You look like you're falling ill."

Amma says I look feverish, too. She lays a hand
on my forehead. Declares, "It's not warm, but perhaps
you should rest anyway. And . . .
here's some momentous news to cheer you up.

"The astrologer I told you of has discovered
that, in just a few months, there will be an auspicious
conjunction of planets. If you marry
at just the right moment, it will annul
any and every bad influence your birth star may have!"

Sisters and Secrets

Maheshvari disturbs my rest,
spinning around,
her skirts swirling,
yelling, "I'm so happy for you!"

But she stops dead when
she sees my face.

"What's the matter?" Maheshvari
flops onto my bed. Guesses, "You've
already fallen for someone?
Just tell your father who it is.
He wants you to be happy."

"If only it were so easy."

"Oh no! He's not a Brahmin?
Well . . . not an insurmountable problem.
After all, doesn't the Rigveda say—"

"Xiang," I whisper. "It's Xiang."

"What! What were you thinking?"

I wasn't thinking.

"It's my fault! I teased you
about him."

"Not your fault."

"He admires you, clearly, but—
he's a Buddhist, and a mleccha!"

I hate the way she spits out the word
foreigner.

"Your brain is so brilliant!
How could your heart be so foolish?"

I try to speak, but my voice
chokes with unshed tears.

She stops scolding and pulls me
into a tight hug. "Sorry. I know
we don't control our hearts."

Amma's Wisdom

Amma invites me to walk with her
to the temple, just her and me.

"Leela," she says, "before
you leave our home,
I want to share with you
one piece of wisdom.
Don't depend on anyone else,
not even your future husband,
to supply your soul's nourishment."

One Last Time

"May we walk together, lady?"
Xiang asks.

I tell Lokasamudra to wait in the library
while Xiang and I dare to stroll the grounds

unchaperoned. I couldn't care less about gossip or propriety.
Xiang is the only man I want to marry.

As soon as we're out of earshot
of anyone else, I blurt it all out.

I have no time to waste
dithering.

Xiang's eyes fill with tears.
He bows his head.

"Leela," he says. "There are many ways to meditate:
movement, stillness, and sometimes, merely the presence
of something that inspires awe.
Or someone whose soul distills the light divine.
You have been a meditation to me.

I admire you as one admires a muse.
I respect you as one respects a teacher.
I shall think of you as one thinks of a lifelong friend.
And I will not lie, lady. When I came to your land,
I was certain I wanted to become a monk.
In our time together I have wondered
if I ought to change course.
To become a husband. Your husband. I dreamed of that honor."

He is speaking the words I dreamed of.
For a second my spirit takes flight.
But when I listen to his tone, my heart
flutters with fear, not delight.

"Leela, if I were to ask for your hand, what could I offer you?
A perilous journey back to a strange land?
Unwelcoming in-laws?"

"You could stay," I find the power to say.
"You could make Ujjayani your home."

"I have considered and reconsidered that as well. But
after my twin died,
I asked myself so many questions. I have begun
unearthing answers
in the Buddha's teachings. I found solace in seeking
knowledge at this university, in . . . you, lady,
but my future lies
in a monastery, in serving others.
Forgive me, wise soul, for my failings."

"You have taken no vow yet.
You are still free to choose.
To choose me!" I sound angry, not sad.

"Please," he begs.
"Please understand.
I will leave
a piece of my heart here
when I return to my homeland.
But return I must."

Rejection

Am I surprised? Dejected? Do I try to persuade
him? No.

After all, I am the unlucky one. And by now
I know

he will not change his mind. He will leave
me alone

again,
like I always
was before.
Like I expected
to be all my life.

Torn Apart

I don't shy away from letting him see
my pain streaming down my cheeks.

He reaches out as if to wipe my tears.
The tip of his finger brushes my cheek.

Then we both pull away.

Wishes

"I love you, lady." His voice shakes. "I do love you,
as much as I can,
but I cannot love you
the way you desire and deserve
the way you may demand a husband love a wife.

"May you always draw strength from this soil.
May you tower over the other teachers of this land.
May you find joy and contentment and peace.
May you marry a man who is as strong and steadfast
in his dedication to you as I hope to remain
in the vows I will take when I join the family of monks."

Marriage Preparations

"We have found a wonderful match," Amma says.
"Gopala! Remember him? You and he and Maheshvari
used to play together when you all were little.
His mother is a lovely, kind woman.
Best of all, they live in Ujjayani, too!"

I try to be happy. I wear a smile and walk through
each day thinking of all that I am lucky to have.

My life becomes dull repetition,
as endless as the division of one by three.

My Groom

Gopala is
no stranger.

He is kind and honest and intelligent and good.
He is handsome and strong and loyal.
His eyes will not rove. His heart will not roam.
Any girl would be delighted to marry him.
Any girl except me.

Perhaps a day will come
when women will wield books
without raising eyebrows
when women will raise children
and
become respected teachers
without raising eyebrows.

That day that I yearn for seems further away
as my impending marriage
looms closer.

Excitement

Lokasamudra is thrilled about my wedding.
He loves tasting the sweets, loves all the food
Amma starts preparing.

He's fascinated by the water clock
Appa has set up to ensure Gopala and I tie the knot
at the perfect time, in the narrow permissible interval,
during the few moments when the heavenly bodies
are in the right spaces to counteract the bad luck
brought by my birth star.

Maheshvari is unduly subdued
after my parents and Gopala's parents meet and agree
on the date and time of the ceremony.

My turn to ask her what's wrong.
"It's just . . . " She chews her lip. "I—I used to
imagine—daydream—being married to Gopala.
When we were children."

What?

"Don't worry. It's not as if we were in love.
It was just—childish. And I'm so
glad for you. You know I'll treat him
with the respect due a brother, once he's your husband."

My turn to hug her.
She rests her head on my shoulder but
holds back her tears.

Suddenly, I see
she's stronger than me.
Could I have been so loving?
So forgiving?

Duties

It's my duty to marry

the man my family has chosen.

If I had an objection,

I ought to have raised it discreetly

long before the date was set.

But is it not my duty

to be honest

with Gopala and

my own self?

Water Clock

Lokasamudra is thrilled
he'll be watching and waiting
to tell us when the moment arrives.

Appa shows us the water clock he's created:
elaborate, accurate, complex.
A system of bowls and rings, designed
to tell time better than a sundial.

Time is   of the essence.
Time is   dripping away . . .

Last Day of Freedom

I visit the library,
run my fingers
over rough palm-leaf pages.

My scholarly life will slowly
melt into nothingness.

Perhaps Gopala will allow his wife—
No. Good man he might be, but I
cannot give him the power to suppress or
permit me to pursue my dreams.

I want to keep learning
the way
I've always done.
I want to keep reading.
I want to keep teaching.

I want to scream.

I shall please, Goddess Saraswathi, help me
I will somehow
I must prevent the nightmare of marriage
to a man I don't love.

Night Before My Wedding

I'm watching the water clock,
counting down to the "auspicious moment"
when I will be forced to marry the wrong man,
when an idea enters my mind.

It's a plan that could easily go awry.
But it's the only plan I have.

"Lokasamudra?" I place a henna-decorated
finger on my lips. "I need your help."

My little brother and I steal
away to the room where the water clock
waits to determine my fate.

"If that hole is plugged,
it will hardly be noticeable, and yet
this clock will no longer be accurate. Correct?"

"Yes. Why?" Lokasamudra watches intently

as I unthread a tiny pearl
from the string Amma gave me to wear tomorrow.

"I need you to slide this pearl into the water clock
to block the flow so it doesn't tell time correctly.
I want you to wait until you are sure
the auspicious moment is long gone and then
come out and tell everyone you spotted it too late."

My little brother's eyes grow large.
"Don't . . . don't you want your marriage to be lucky?
Why would you want me to do that?
Amma will be so sad.
Appa will be so angry!"

"Appa's anger is like thunderclouds that blow away
before rain falls from them. He might rage at us—at me—
but he'd never hurt a hair on our heads. I'll say I came
alone to look at the clock because I was curious and the pearl
fell out somehow
unnoticed. I'll make sure
he won't blame you."

"He won't believe you."

Lokasamudra's answer says I can trust him.
Lokasamudra's answer promises he'll do the favor I ask of him.
"Someday, when you're older, I'll tell you why
I needed to stop this wedding. And
every day of my life, I'll thank you. I promise."

Time

Will Appa check the water clock and catch sight of my pearl?
Will Lokasamudra do everything correctly?

Please let the crucial few moments
when the planets are properly aligned for my marriage
slip irretrievably away, unnoticed as my parents
welcome wedding guests and bustle about
with wedding arrangements.
Help me, Goddess Saraswathi,
Goddess of Learning, help me stay unwed like you!
Please let my plan succeed.
Please let me be free to lead
my life
my way.

Past

Lokasamudra rushes in. "I'm sorry!
I didn't see there was a pearl
blocking the flow of water in the clock.
I'm scared the special moment is gone!"

Appa rushes out, returning to say,
"The time of perfect planetary alignment is over.
Leela cannot marry now."
Amma begins to cry.

"Let me speak to Leela," Gopala demands.
"Alone. For just a moment."
The two of us step aside.

"Leela, I do not care about the stars.
Your family has gone to great expense and trouble.
I will not disappoint them. Or break my promise to you.
I will see this wedding through." Gopala's kindness wins
my admiration. Truly.
But my heart is Xiang's alone. "Gopala, how can I wed you now?

If anything happened, I would
blame myself for endangering you. But . . . if I may be so bold,
would you consider
marrying Maheshvari?"

Gopala

The crowd babbles in confusion
when Gopala asks to marry Maheshvari
instead of me.

His mother agrees immediately. "Of course.
She is just as pretty and intelligent as Leela."

"But what about her stars?"
his father asks.

"Their star charts match. Perfectly,"
I whisper to Appa. "I checked."

Appa stares at me
the way he looks
at an equation before
arriving at the answer.

He repeats my words aloud.

Lokasamudra's eyes dart about like bees
as he tries to take it all in.

In his curious face I see children I
never will have. The mother I will never be.

Maheshvari's arched eyebrows
shoot silent questions at me.

I answer her with my smile.

She hugs me tight and this time,
when we break apart,

my shoulder is wet with her tears.

The Wedding

Maheshvari takes my place beside Gopala.
She repeats the wedding vows
with an earnest eagerness
I could never match.

Evening

Tears drip down my cheeks
like water in the clock
as I watch Maheshvari depart
from our family home.

We've parted ways
on life's road. She's leaving another
empty space in my heart.

Her path is filled with family and friends,
companionship and connection.
Each step I take on my as-yet-untrodden path
will make me more and more alone.
Or perhaps
I can invent a new place for myself?
Won't I be teacher and aunt, writer and sister?
Can't I laugh with Lokasamudra's wife and play with his children,
even as I teach at the university and help Appa write his tomes?

Appa's Request

"If you had married," Appa says,
"your name would have blurred, just as a dot in a kolam
becomes part of the line the artist draws through it.
Unmarried, your name will be yours
forever. And, if you wish, we will make your name immortal."

He places a writing nail in my hand.
"Will you help me write my next treatise?
I want to name it after you."

Even as he asks me,
even as I accept, I wonder:
How many men will acknowledge my right to authorship?

How many years before they decide
Lilavathi was written by Bhaskaracharya alone?
How many women before me
have been veiled by the mists of time?

Will there ever come a day when someone
wonders if I was a mathematician in my own right?
Will anyone ever seek my name,
my story?

Prayer

My soul fills with resolve.
My heart leaps with ideas.
My hand is steady.

Like the lighthouse sculpted from granite that blazes
night after night atop a lonely hill in Mamallapuram,

gazing upon an empty sea, waiting to guide lost
ships to safe harbor,

I pray the book bearing my name will brighten
a path for other women to follow.
Numbers flow
through my mind,
and my fingers

shape them into poetry on the palm-leaf page.

Letter from Xiang

Lady, it has been long
since our last meeting.
But I have seen you often
in my mind and heart.

And today I carried
the volume that carries
your name in my hands.

If you had married a good man,
as I hoped you would,
I might never have met
the children of your flesh.

I am grateful I could meet
the child of your mind:
this book I'll be able to hold forever.

May this book ignite the flame
of your passion for mathematics
in many men and women.

May the fire of your first love
remain immortal,
as does my respect and admiration
for you.

I remain, your friend
forever.

America Through Mistranslation: A Heart Map of Scars

By Eric Gansworth

You Have Heard This Before

from a thousand different Indian families.
It always starts the same, a rough map
labeled: *You Are Here.* The legend: *1/7 Scale:*
Survival Measured One Generation to Seven Beyond.
Sometimes a legend tells a story and sometimes
a legend tells the scale, and sometimes a legend
allows you to see two images at once.

It begins with a government agent showing up
on the reservation like a nightmare. The twentieth
century had not yet arrived, so most people
had never seen a car, a future metallic insect grown
to monstrous size. The agents, pale, said, "If you love
your children enough to give them a future, you will
let me carry them away to be prepared," but my great-
grandparents learned English haphazardly, imperfectly
working in the city, only as much as they needed,
bringing it home in small, inexact fragments to spread
among those who spoke only Tuscarora, and eventually
their generation thought in two languages simultaneously.

Together they invented new words for unfamiliar things
and obscured words for ideas they thought risky for their
children's futures, to be released as needed. They had one
advantage. English is based in nouns and Tuscarora
is built on verbs—action, not object. Imagine love
is a verb, and verbs are the building blocks, action

revealing desperate need. They felt compelled to let
their children depart for the future in the metal
insect and hoped their actions would lead those
children home with tools for themselves and others.

They know tools, with slight shifts of intention, can become
weapons and that the best weapons are ones we can hide. But
sometimes we forget where we buried them. Because we hid
the old love words, we make new ones to replace the losses.
Every new expression would be crafted keeping silent action
and reaction in mind so no outsider could find
these tools and potentially use them against us.

My grandmother would eventually imagine love was
an act of growing, defined in this strip of land large
enough to sustain generations of imagination,
originating in this spot, and we all recognize it
by the clear-cutting, and all the scars left behind.

Identity Theft

Two generations later, I think in English—
Tuscarora remains in necessary brain slivers. By my
time, the patch of land my grandmother considered
her universe held three homes, for three of her
children. She knew one would inherit her house and more
generations would come, trusting the land would help
us remember who we were. She knew this information had
been stolen from us before and needed to be recovered.

My grandmother mapped numerous routes, in case
we needed to find our way home, tattooing a reservation
map on our hearts, each beat toughening the scar.

She didn't know the word *metaphor* but
she knew her husband made it home from
the boarding school, hundreds of miles
away, trying to rewrite the scar map of
his heart, and in her steely way, she reminded
him of their parallel paths and eventual crossroads.

He tried to put her land in his name, but she
suspected love would take her only so far. He believed
in America and its promise. She had taken his name
and church, losing her own, but her children would inherit
only his name. In America, the man ruled the household,
but the reservation looked like America only from
the outside. The land was hers and would become
theirs only if they remembered the Legend and the way
things in real life are larger than they seem on the page.

The Plot, or Latitudes and Longitudes of Love

My grandmother knew time would unfurl the map
of her love for us, her descendants two generations
later, to rebuild, coax new life from cuttings
and bare roots she left, those her own ancestors
had carried for her, to start in this place, the heart
map of scars so deep, no school designed to scour
memories from its charges would ever find them.

She understood love as a verb still needed
earth to grow. Forced to lose land to New York's
eminent domain, water flooding homelands,
histories, and futures, she bought a piano,
an instrument requiring passion and dedication
to transcend generations. An instrument without
a committed player only plays silent songs of dust

and neglect. But she ensured her children and then her
grandchildren didn't learn drums or rattles. She knew
which instruments were labeled civilized and which were
considered savage. So she blocked this complication in
their lives, remembering the ways history lived in her head and
in her heart, punctured notes on her sharply defined scar maps.

Map lines look direct, clean, informed declarations
of places, but a heart landscape's hills, valleys,
mountains, and caverns shift with tectonic love
songs regularly. Though she preferred the orderly
rows of corn behind her house, she did let wild berries
grow frenzied at field's edge, harvesting to respect nature's
defenses. She savored short seasons growing
at the crossroads of love, dipping deeper dimples.

The piano and all its keys reminded her daily of geography
through experience, her own family plans ripped from her
story without any say. She was reminded that she'd been forced
to give up land she'd set aside for some of her children's futures,
and when the government insisted on eminent-domain claims
and took those parcels anyway, she was left with nothing except
a predetermined number of dollars to fill the map's emptiness.

We Are the Wild

While my parents make sure food is on
the table, my grandparents grow hopes
and plans, earning the luxury to rest and think
about desires instead of doing the next chore.
They have time for these important thoughts,
but mostly they make suggestions and dream
for the best, believe their own children
believe in love action enough to follow
the map drawn from careful observation.

We are raised by these elder dream cartographers,
while our parents ensure food arrives on the table.

And we, the grandchildren, gravitate to our own desires, before maps are offered, following our own magnetic north. We are unaware our grandparents reconciled the needle thrumming our compasses with the creased map our grandmother wanted for us.

I was too young to speak before she left, but if I'd had words, and if I had had awareness in time, I would have wanted to say to her, "Maybe . . ."

Maybe if she'd been born inside the group and
maybe if she hadn't witnessed boarding schools and
maybe if she hadn't watched her land flooded forever and
maybe if she hadn't had cousins her age treated differently and
maybe if she hadn't known this was because of love and
maybe if she hadn't known that struggle was our future too,
maybe she'd have insisted that we be raised like corn . . .
maybe she'd have ripped out those thorny berry whips and
maybe banished their wildness to the woods so
maybe we'd never have gotten ideas about growing wild and
maybe avoiding the cultivation of neat, orderly rows, and
maybe, all this time, she secretly loved the wildness
of berries even more than the orderly rows of obedient,
uniform corn and was smart enough to continue keeping
her reinvented love language within silent bounds she
devised, passing on her invisible plans for us to survive,
untraceable by others, emerging only in our shared actions.

A Quarter

By the time my grandmother left this world,
she had twenty-five grandchildren. It would have
been twenty-six, but one berry had grown wilder

than the others, leaving early and unexpectedly, one
rain-slicked road stripping him of his wildness before
he had fully bloomed to his rightful place, all thorns, buds,
and potential, striving to find his own spot in the sun.

Twenty-five was a good enough number
to leave behind. Even if most of us grew orderly
like corn, she could be confident that each of the rare
thorny berry whips would find at least one among
the other twenty-four. Each would emerge at some point,
to follow or lead, or run parallel lines, weaving
tighter the closer our paths aligned. The more we'd
discover that we wouldn't have to go it alone, the stronger
we'd grow. At least one other wild berry would appear in
the sweep of orderly brothers and sisters and first cousins and
second cousins. At least one other would understand that being
the outsider is a relative state of existence. Maybe in that state,
one wild relative in twenty-four orderly ones would be enough.

Twenty-five possible longitudes run against
my latitude, a quarter of a hundred possibilities,
but the odds of a prime meridian overlapping
my equator are much slimmer than I'd imagined.
Even as she held me on her lap in those final
months of her life, the best she could dream
was that I'd be like most of the others planted
here, on the family plot, or that there would be
at least one other wild whip whose ears were tuned
to the same radio signals my secret antennae received.

The Odds

Because I arrived so late, the chances
of my finding that similar family member

diminished. In the perpetual relative map
of growing up, the more years between
us, the fewer the pathways cross one
another, the fewer connections we have.
Any map with fewer roads inevitably
has fewer other roads to cross and intersect.

When we're all the same, no one notices,
but if you begin exhibiting curious interests,
you are in the spotlight. My siblings knew quickly
that I was different. What were the odds our cousins
would not perceive me like an insect, beneath
a magnifying glass, easy to control, not yet dangerous?
I recognized my difference early but had no choice
except to live out my time, curious features exposed,
sending signals I hoped would find a receiver.

Sah-Lah Disregards the Map

Eight years older, my cousin is by nature inventive,
creating new adventures from abandoned
scraps. He grasps the Way of Things as
little more than a suggestion, a place to step
off from and explore the vast space beyond.

Sah-Lah traded TV, a sound system, and electricity
altogether, leaving his mother's house behind, crowded
with siblings, for wide, solo space without distractions
and luxuries, a place to dream in, the stripped life
of our shared uncle, who had dwelled alone in the third
house on our grandmother's property, at its easternmost
end of the family plot. Our uncle's house is the crossroad
on the map where the only music came from his voice, and
gnarled hands played solo, strumming an ancient six-string.

And because Sah-Lah was already creating his own grooves in the family story, such a leap to another home seemed logical, and though I ask siblings how Sah-Lah changed his residence, made the seismic move, not picturing such a leap myself, no one provides me the clear answer I'm seeking.

I'll never truly understand the map Sah-Lah follows, because he keeps it a secret, one that only he knows how to read. He traces paths that his feet alone will trod, pressing grass and twisting branches subtly, creating maps in the ways of old path makers in case someone might discover the path and follow it. Even I might be able to follow it, should I someday feel I'm up to the task and ambition.

Sah-Lah Reaches for the Sky

Sah-Lah is a man of transformation. He builds and learns to use stilts, towering above us all, like Tallman, the mystery figure who lurks among our shadowed woods. Sah-Lah rises on discarded lumber scraps. He acquires a bullwhip, snapping and cracking it, ripping the sky with sound, years before Indiana Jones blasts into America's big-screen imagination, stealing artifacts from other cultures.

Sah-Lah learns how to construct a kite from basic materials, and one windy day, everyone gathers to watch his first attempt. He holds the kite till exactly the right moment of tension, releasing just as it wants most to fly, and we watch his casually magic hands play the spool he's built, gently keeping tension and string taut, tail dancing and snapping whiplike while the kite climbs higher

and higher, sunlight illuminating its stretched white
surface into a sky diamond fleeing to its own future.

And I wonder if our city cousins could
see it and know we were thinking of them.
Was this kite a flare to help them find their way
home, reweaving threadbare map connections
they'd gripped fiercely for years?

Of course, his tether string took the kite
just so far, and he gracefully brought
it home without crashing. Only years later
did I understand the kite danced strictly
for our small gathering of cousins,
Sah-Lah's intimate symphony of skies
and all the ways we were tied to home.

The Lure of Fifty Cents an Hour

isn't much, even in 1972. Already at seven,
I've run through a series of babysitters
with my strange and insistent interests,
my inability to be tricked or coerced
into what they've wanted me to do.

But my next-door cousins are plentiful, and
Sah-Lah, at fifteen, is also in his own orbit.
Too young for his older siblings, too old to be
a kid, he tries sending broad signals. A seven-
year-old is hardly the best cousin for him to hang
with, but even at seven, I'm the only cousin in
walking distance tuned to his eccentric signals.

Sah-Lah has dreams, and understands he will have
to find his own ways to further them. He keeps

an eye on me for fifty cents an hour instead
of hanging out with friends, breaking rules of cool
for fifteen-year-old boys, performing a job his friends
would have refused. He understands sacrifice and patience.

Watching Him Watching You Smudge

The two of us, alone in my mother's house, celebrate
electricity. Sah-Lah, used to the dark, luxuriates
in our bright, triple-bulb overhead fixture, the wide
expanse of dining room table below, illuminated as if
for surgery. And I can watch his magic firsthand.

Officially he is babysitting me. He silences
the perpetual TV, and the two of us agree
on music. Because I am seven, others never
ask, but he listens, and the night music belongs
to both of us, and if he hates the suggestions
I've made with his invitation, he doesn't say.

He removes a portrait from our wall, my
niece, the first baby of the next generation.
Propping it on the table, he reveals a spiral
pad of thick, textured drawing paper, raised
like a desert topographical map, and black pencils
with lead so dark, they seem like a million night skies
gathered in one place. He explains they are charcoal
as he retrieves a knife and gently shaves two to graceful
points, like arrows, showing me secret codes marked
on the ends, *HB*, *6B*, *4B*, like the paper type, named
in the closed language of artists I've never heard.

By then, I've already been told I hold my pen wrong
in school over and over, as if there is only one way

to grip, as if I were not already making drawings
others could recognize without my having to tell them.

I immediately notice Sah-Lah's big, graceful lines
across the page, suggestions, and smaller, softer faint
whispers inside. The page miraculously hints at my
niece in Sah-Lah's gestures. So magic, I almost forget
to notice he holds his pencil differently, his hand removed
from the paper at all times, floating above, a kite caught
on a wind so high humans can't feel it, taking him away.

But that night, as Sah-Lah performs magic
at the dining room table for me, an audience of
one, he reveals miracles, too, adding those magic
words: "You wanna try?" Carefully tearing a sheet
of thick, textured paper from his pad, he sharpens
another mysterious night-sky pencil, conjured from
the past remnants of fires in some faraway place,
pressed into the service of his vision and now into yours.

In this way, he invites you to dream side by side
and join him in drawing new maps that don't
necessarily involve pain and scars left behind as reward.

He rests the pencil, washes his hands, slides them down his
pant legs till they dry, and, with one index finger, touches
the ghost lines and gestures, an intentional charcoal smudge,
like a carpenter, confident about the beginning and ending
of each line, and in every new exacting sweep, my niece's
face becomes so alive, I almost hear her laugh captured on film.

Paper-Bag Drawer

When I'm allowed to go to the store,
I request a BIC pen and a pad of paper,

blank. Used to "no," I still dream "yes,"
and express my desires clearly in case.

At first, I inherit pens missing caps
and paper grocery bags, gutted to reveal
tan, blank innards, so all my drawings
arrive blotched with drying ink in perpetual
twilight. I am told these bags could be used for
other things, but that instead, I am allowed
to waste them. My family does not understand
that, by seven, I already grasp that monthly
groceries are a finite commodity, never
arriving in the desired amount and quality.

Careful, I still know my drawings
don't look right, but the origins of my
mistakes are unclear, even as I stare,
hoping someone will speak. All choose
silence, but only I know that I don't seek
praise and instead want answers, keys, legends.

Heroes

While Sah-Lah draws my niece, practicing
exact hand-eye coordination, I am stuck
with the blunt fine motor skills of a kid, annoyed
my hand has not caught up with my brain.

I balance my hand above, attempt techniques
my brain sees but my eyes can't translate,
language lost or not yet gained. My figures keel,
lopsided, wounded by my unskilled hand, but
I follow the magic Sah-Lah has shown, washing
my hands and smudging them across the paper.

Though we both draw family, mine seem pained,
off-kilter and fragile, distorted. Maybe my drawings
captured the fragments of my grandparents' history.
At boarding school, they had only themselves, each
other, shared memories to rescue them from the burning
libraries of history where they'd stored their words for love.

As with so many lessons, I have learned this
one poorly and incompletely. I will know one
day some Indians smudge to heal and move on, but
I am not there yet, left bereft, with merely a dirty,
ruined sheet of Sah-Lah's sacrificed beautiful paper.

And as hopeless as it seems, Sah-Lah reveals another
tool, closer to medicine than magic, a kneaded
eraser, which he squeezes and twists and softens,
then shows me how it lifts smudges I don't want,
warning me to be careful and not remove the smudges
I do want. He lets me understand how light and dark
work together and reminds me that time will be my biggest
tool in helping me find my heroes, when my muscles
and eyes and brain and bones will all work in concert.
There is no shortcut on the long stretching road of time,
patience, practice, and a belief in finding the maps in scars.

Darkness Grows Back One Dot at a Time

We age at the same pace,
but Sah-Lah will always be
eight years older, almost
a generation of experience ahead
when I am young, granting
me a preview, of pen and ink,
thick nibs and impossibly small
ones, like ink needles, bleeding

an image one tiny dot at a time,
and as I practice, he gives me
the magic word: *stipple*. Each mark
a singular spot on paper, shadows
growing only as the spots accumulate
in greater number, fading fainter
the farther from each other they fall,
each dot losing its power in isolation.

This feels like a metaphor, a word
I now know. The further I go
into the white world, the less present
my identity seems to become, the lighter
my accent sounds until it is mostly gone except
when perched at Friday-evening home bonfires,
generating ashes and charcoal into the night.

A rich and varied stipple requires patience
and concentration, in short supply when I
am ten and he is eighteen, beginning to show
me techniques he learns in his brief flirtation
with college before turning to roofing. He allows
me to see the hard choice of paying tuition with
money he doesn't have, or making car payments
to drive to work so he can afford his car payments.

As We Float Higher than Roofs

Sah-Lah paints in his free time, but how much is
free at day's end, when he pounds shingle
layers, hours on end, to keep the rain out
of someone else's roof and a stable shelter
above his own head, and his own drawing table?

With my first summer paycheck, the year I'm fourteen,
I ask him to share his knowledge of oil paint, the only
artist I know who leaped from thought to action, following
his ideas floating untethered higher before they grew too
distant and disappeared. I'm interested in practical matters.
The reality of paint and brushes starting at five dollars apiece
in the store overwhelms, implies I'll need years to accrue
colors and tools to dream in color, the way I want to.

He says in his short college career, he bought
paint, brushes, and turpentine, with financial aid.
But the thought of college is a blank canvas to me.

Our grandmother's plan awakens intact, collective
memory for Sah-Lah and for me arriving later, to find
each other. He sells me his paints for twenty dollars,
including a couple of stiffened brushes, if I'm dedicated
enough to revive them, with patience and concentration.

I ask what he'll use, and he says he spends
too much time in the sky all day to worry about
reaching clouds long enough to dream. And I say
any time he wants some back for a new painting,
I am, as always, just two houses away, completing
our grandmother's dreams of legacy. As I paint, my
mother perches at my grandmother's Lost Land piano
thinking she's alone. She plays for the joy of creation,
melody and counterpoint carrying all of us higher.

The Vast Limits of Land and Imagination

One day, Sah-Lah will be a grandfather
and my niece will become a grandmother,

but at fourteen, making my first painting
across my bedroom wall, I cannot comprehend
the way life will stretch past endless sunrises
and sunsets on this epic land on bonfire nights.
I will not spend every night here, sleeping
beneath the roof my grandfather secured
in my grandmother's name for me.

That house, like so many things, will vanish
in flames, taking that first oil painting
with it, blackening the air with my family
history, with smoke so thick, even a kite would
lose its way without a map and a steady hand.

Love as a verb is a song and a painting.
It stretches across generations, signals
sent, received in nouns and verbs mixing
survival languages imperfectly on a heart
map and its legend. Awaiting new ears,
it offers a future home to seek within
the confines of its scar-toughened borders
whenever someone needs directions home.

Kaleidoscope

By Alexandra Alessandri

Bursting to Be Free

A new day awakens
wide and bright and
bursting with the promise
of change.

It's the first day
of my first job,
and like a seed
that's been buried
for too long, I'm
bursting to be free.

I fly out of Mami's car,
heart spread wide
and smile stretched thin

while worry wiggles
below my breastbone:
    what if I'm buried
    once more?

Mami Worries Too

Before we left the house, Mami paced
rivers on the rug because maybe
she shouldn't have said yes.

It's too soon.

She worries about my readiness and
steadiness after all these years of
slowing down so I could heal.

You're not ready.

She worries about the taxes and tolls
a new job will claim on my body,
and whether it's worth it at all.

Maybe next year.

She worries I haven't healed from
that day, from the accident that
left me shattered and empty.

Remember your fibromyalgia.

As if I could forget. When I
can't stand Mami's pacing
any longer, I whisper,

Chill, Mom. It'll be fine.

What I Don't Say

Is I'm scared to be in that place   again,
a shell of a girl   drowning in pain and fatigue
and a fog so dense   I barely break the surface.

Because I *know* this job could shatter me
even more, but Catalina would've wanted me
to bloom.

I'm scared that strangers will learn my weakness
and shut me out the way my friends did—
or worse scatter pity over my brokenness.
(Because no one knows what to do with a girl
who's been cursed by chronic illness
and grief.)

But I'm even more scared
of not living
my life.

Call Me Sarai

Mami tells me
my name means
princesa
but it's also
a name of resilience
and overcoming.

I've wished so much
for this to be true,
but all I've been able to do
since Catalina died
is survive.

But here,
standing beneath
Farmacia Navarro's
neon-blue signs,

I'm finally
ready
to live.

Catalina

My sister would've been nineteen this month,
growing and glowing like a luciérnaga,
on her way to college.

FSU, pre-pharmacy, top of her class.

Instead, she's in St. Andrews Cemetery.
The same accident that crushed my body
three years ago claimed her life.

She was the same age I am now—

excited and eager behind the wheel
(without Mami for the first time).
Someone ran the red light.

We never saw it coming.

My world hasn't been the same since,
but I made a promise after she died
to hit all the milestones she missed.

This job   today
is me keeping my promise to my sister.

Few Things Scream Miami

Like the Cuban-owned pharmacy
and mercado
near my house, filled with
Agua de Violetas,

pastelitos and cafecitos,
and panetones during the holidays.
Spanish rolls through the aisles
in waves,
comforting and soothing.

I'm not Cuban—
I'm Colombian American—
but still, I feel at home here.
It's bold and bright and happy.

If only   my heart
would stop galloping,
jittery and afraid
that my attempt
at keeping promises

will fail.

I Meet

My manager Santiago
and Rosita the pharmacist,
wave hello and smile shyly
to the other workers:
Martica and Caleb,
cashiers like me,
and Mauro and Suzi,
roaming the aisles.

Then there's Josue,
whose smile
is like the sun.

My Trainer Josue

Reminds me
of Catalina—
      kind eyes
      easy smile
      down to business.
He's her age too,
or how old she would be
if she were still alive.

Our fingers brush as
Josue hands me
a blue shirt and
bright orange name tag
with Sarai González
printed in bold block letters
      (they even got
      the accent right),
and for a moment I wonder
what Catalina would think
if she saw me.

But I chase the thought away.
Instead, I shadow Josue as he
trains me to
      check in
      use the register
      stock shelves
until my nerves
settle into a
familiar rhythm

until I can't help
the thought that unfurls:
He's cute.

It's Complicated

While Josue trains me,
he asks me questions:
How old are you?
Where's school for you?
His gaze is steady,
expression open as he
leans in for my response.
I try to tightrope the line
between truth and TMI.

Truth: *I'm sixteen.*

Truth: *It's complicated.*

TMI: I'm homeschooled because
after the accident, Mami
couldn't bear
        to see me struggle at school
couldn't bear
        to be separated from me
couldn't bear
        to lose another daughter.
So Mami kept me home.
Truth be told, the pain and fatigue
kept me home anyway,
no matter how much I wished to go back.

No one wants to hear that, though—
it's too messy and broken and sad.
I learned that the hard way,
when friends fell away like
sand through my fingertips.

Which is why I don't tell Josue
any of that.

Customers

Two hours into my shift
customer after customer comes my way
while Josue hovers by my register,
smelling of bubblemint gum.
We make small talk in between,
and I find myself bending toward him
as if he were the sun.

Three hours into my shift
customer after customer brings offerings
and I find my fingers faltering,
my brain slowing
as I will myself
to catch up
to stay focused
on what I'm supposed to do.

Four hours into my shift
customer after customer
smiles politely
taps impatiently
checks their watch and waits
for me to ring their merchandise
correctly, while Josue
catches my mistakes,
never breaking his stride.

Me, though,
I find myself

losing my rhythm,
wishing I could speed
to the end of my shift
(two more hours)
so I can go home and reset.

But at least
I'm not flaring
                    (yet).

FLARING

\ 'fler-iŋ \
Adjective:

In autoimmune diseases,
or chronic illnesses
like mine,
when symptoms
increase,
flare up,
get worse.

And it feels
like that time
when I was little
swimming
in South Beach,
angry waves
knocking me down,
tumbling me over, and I

couldn't
seem to catch

my breath
between breaks.

Before / After

Before the accident,
I played soccer
competitively,
and the promise
of high school
bloomed bright
like Mami's girasoles.

After the accident,
days bled into nights

in wave

after wave

of pain

fatigue

fog

and I lay unable to break
the surface and breathe.

Now I inhabit
some space
between
healing
and hell.

Fibromyalgia

Can creep up on you suddenly
after a cataclysmic event—
like the crash that nearly killed you

or the grief of losing your sister,
your best friend,
the brightest star in the universe

  or both things at once.

And it won't ever go away.

What They Don't Tell You

Is that when you get sick
you'll spend
days
weeks
months
years
measuring your worth
with
good days
and bad days
or that you'll learn
every creak
snap
pop
ache of
your body,
always
anticipating
another flare-up.

Like now,
I watch the clock
tick toward the end
of my shift,
feel a burn in my limbs,
and wonder
if this is just
new-work tired
or a crash
waiting
to happen.

Doña Adelita

Fifteen minutes
before I finish,
a woman walks in—
silver hair,
joyful laugh,
and a lightness about her
that draws me in.
If Josue is the sun,
then she is a brilliant star.

Hola, Doña Adelita,
Josue calls out.
Doña Adelita waves,
catches my eye, and winks.
She floats over to us,
says, *You're new.*

I am.
Is it that obvious?

How wonderful,
Doña Adelita trills.
I'll be sure to check out
with you.

As Promised

Doña Adelita
ambles into my aisle,
places ice packs and
lipstick and
merenguitos
on the counter.

While I scan,
she fiddles
with her wallet,
her curled fingers slipping
on the clasp
until finally
it opens with a click.

She glances at my name tag
as she hands me the cash.

Sarai.
Beautiful name
for a beautiful girl.

I smile and thank her,
though truth be told
it's hard to feel beautiful
when you can't

see yourself clearly
through the shattered glass,
when scars remind you
of all you're not.

She begins chatting
with Josue

about college
    freshman year
    studying biomedical engineering
about family
    sister graduating
    Mom away on business
about me
    Seems just your type.
    Don't you think?

Josue's face flushes,
my eyes widen, and
Doña Adelita's laugh trails behind her
as she leaves—

and I can't help but wonder
if he agrees.

What It Feels Like to Be Free

When my six-hour shift ends,
I find Mami waiting for me
in the car, her face lined with
expectation and worry,
a contrast to my own
smiling, glowing face.

How'd it go? she asks.

Fine.

Better than fine.
Sure, exhaustion blankets me
now as we drive home,
and sure, my body aches
with the exertion of the day,
but I'm giddy with the thought that

I didn't fail.

And I feel my heart
flowering from the splinters
that still lie scattered and broken.

I'd forgotten what it feels like
to be like everyone else,

what it feels like to be free.

My Routine

Includes
meds,
rest,
yoga,
light exercise
to keep
my body
moving, loose,
so when the flare

becomes a hurricane,
my body
can withstand it.

It's not a perfect system,
but I've learned
to go with the sway
of the waves,
even while I dream
of calmer waters.

So tonight, I take my
meds, do some yoga to
s t r e t c h
my sore muscles, and tuck
into bed to rest, hoping
to keep the good times

rolling.

But I don't sleep
all that well.

Doña Adelita Visits

Farmacia Navarro every day.
She only buys a few things at a time—
pantyhose,
shampoo,
merenguitos
        (always
        merenguitos).
She flutters through the aisles

like a colibrí searching
for flowers,
her trilling laughter
always trailing
behind her,
and when she's done,
she always checks out
with me.

And while I scan her items,
she starts chatting

about life
    it's just me
    and Mami (now)
about school
    I'll finish
    ahead of schedule
about me
    Why do you look like the weight
    of the world is on your shoulders?

It's hard to stay quiet around Doña Adelita
because the gleam in her gaze
tells me she *knows.*

But I do

because Josue lingers nearby,
and some truths are just too much

to share with a boy
you think is
cute.

If I Could Respond, This Is What I'd Say

This weight you see me carrying
is my fractured world in my arms,
no longer whole, just broken glass
and a sister-sized piece missing.

This weight you see me carrying
is my mom's grief, which multiplies
like weeds, seeds dispersing until
all joy and beauty are snuffed out.

This weight you see me carrying
is me wondering if it's possible
to build a mosaic from
all these scattered pieces.

Catalina and I

The way Mami tells it, we were
inseparable from the moment I was born—
me, the sister she'd always wished for,
and she, the sister I always needed.
From lazy summers and telenovelas
to late-night study sessions and
ice cream binges after heartaches

We were a pair   Catalina and I   me and Catalina

I wanted to be just like my sister,
studious, bubbly, kind, determined.
Catalina never stopped, hands moving,
mind grinding, always planning.

She had big dreams—to make
medicine more affordable for everyone—
and even though I was fine living in her shadow,
she pushed me to bloom.

Without her now, I must remind myself
to keep on dreaming for the two of us,
to keep on trying to grow something beautiful
from the ruins, but I don't know how
to do life without her.

Everyone Has a Story

And I wonder
about Doña Adelita's.
She always comes in
alone,
the weight of age
in the lines of her face,
in the fumbling of her fingers,
but she moves
with quiet dignity
and joy.

I wonder
if, like Mami, she left
her home across the sea
or if she has family
nearby—
a spouse,
children,
grandchildren,
even great-grandchildren.

I wonder
if she ever minds
being alone
and if not,
I wonder if
I'll ever
get there too.

Josue Takes the Day Off

Leaving me to fend for myself,
and for a moment, I feel suspended
before an abyss, waiting
for the moment when I

f

a

l

l

but I don't. I settle
into polite smiles and
conversations about weather,
candles and birthday parties,
my fingers now familiar
with the keys of the register,
with the rhythm of checking out.

Martica shares her cafecito,
and Suzi deals some pastelitos
to Rosita and Caleb,

to Mauro, my manager, and me.
The only member
I'm missing is Josue—
with his hovering and
bubblemint scent
and smile that feels like home.

Catalina would be proud of me.
She always said I was
too shy   too much
of an introvert, and here I am
making small talk like a pro.
I wish she could see me now.

But she can't, and
the thought leaves my heart
splintered and bruised.

When Doña Adelita Visits While Josue Is Away

I feel emboldened, eager to ask the questions
that otherwise sit in my belly, like indigestion.
Perhaps it's her openness, the soft lines
on her face that sketch a story I wish to know.
Perhaps it's an ache for the abuela I never knew.
Either way, I start off slow.
What's so special about merenguitos anyway?

Her laugh tinkles as she shakes her bag of
merenguitos, says they're heaven's sugar, that's for sure.

I laugh alongside her,
then ask what I *really* want to know.
Tell me about your family.

Her smile falters as she says,
I'm all that's left.

Parents gone.
Husband gone.
Children gone.

Never had any grandchildren.

I've never wished to take questions back
the way I do right now.

But still, something about
the slump of her shoulders,
the shadows in her gaze
(which remind me so much
of my own reflection),
makes me ask,

What happened?

Her eyes take on that faraway look people get
when they're remembering.

Carbon monoxide poisoning.
I wasn't home when it happened,
had gone out shopping for hours,
and when I came back,
they were gone.

We stand there, lost in the silence
of her memory, until Doña Adelita asks,

How about you? Who did you lose?

The question stills me.
How did you know?

Doña Adelita pats my hand,
says,
    Sometimes grief finds a mirror
    in someone else's sorrow.

I let her words settle in my heart
until I can't help but spill my truth.

Who Did I Lose?

My sister,
my sunshine,
my hero,
the one who shone
brighter than a firefly,
who left a black hole
when she flew back home,
wherever that is.

How do you get back to a place
of living,   of love,
when the one you loved most
is no longer with you?

Doña Adelita's Wisdom

You never truly forget them, but you
learn to live with their memory,
learn to count your heartbeats,
reminding you that you're still alive,
and life, like the living, is a gift.

But what if that memory
keeps me gripped beneath waves
so I'm drowning again and again?

You learn to find beauty in the ashes,
to choose joy in the hard places,
to make art from broken pieces,
to become a kaleidoscope, reflecting
a rainbow from your pain.

What if the best I can do is walk
barefoot through the smoke-filled forests
of my mind? What if I never find beauty again?

You learn to love the world
fully wildly unabashedly
to make up for all the love
you had left to give.

What if all the love I had left to give
is buried in St. Andrews Cemetery, with
my sister? What if I've shriveled up and dried?

You learn to live life on your own
and to offer yourself grace
when you fall down the well of
remembering and missing and grieving
because that will never truly go away.

I don't know if I can.

I'm Not a Kaleidoscope

I'm just broken glass
scattered on an empty lot,

forgotten,
a nuisance to those

who walk over me, their feet
crunching over my brokenness.

I'm just sharp edges
and hard angles.

Dull, scratched, shattered—
I'm not a kaleidoscope

at all.

But I don't tell Doña Adelita this.
I simply smile sadly, finish ringing her
up, and watch her walk slower than usual to her car.

When Josue Returns

So does the sun, bright and warm
like his smile.

He lingers by my register,
shares some pastelitos
with me, and I wonder
what it might be like
to know him better.

But what would a boy want
with a shattered girl
who can't reflect
his light?

The Crash Doesn't Come Right Away

It builds

slowly,

pressure

growing,

each day

checking off

one more

symptom.

First is

exhaustion

as I push

to keep my

promise

to my

sister

and myself

(even though I should know better
than to push myself when I'm down).

Then

brain fog

drifts in,

gradually

making

me fumble

with math

at my register.

(Thank God for Josue, who
keeps me from floating away.)

Finally,

the pain

hits hard

and fast,

a tornado

within

this Cat 5

hurricane,

and I’m

trapped

at home

once more.

I Hate My Life

Sometimes,
my life is
pity parties—
sad violins
and trombones.

Mami throws out
her *I told you so*s
faster than the güiros
of her favorite cumbias,
but I try
to tune her out,
try to tell myself
this is just
a small hiccup
in keeping
my promise.

I’ll get
back to work
(back to Josue)
soon.
I have to.

I Call In Sick

For the rest of the week,
feel the pain and fatigue
mingle with the missing
of my Farmacia Navarro family,

especially Josue.
(Does he miss me too?)

I hear Mami on the phone with
my manager Santiago,
feel the shame when she asks
for special accommodations

even though all I want
is to be like everyone else,

even though I know
I'm not like everyone else.

My brain *knows* I shouldn't feel ashamed,
but my heart can't help what it feels.

Josue Texts

You okay?
I asked Santiago
for your number.
You've been
gone so long,
and Doña Adelita
keeps asking

about you.

I wonder if
that's true
or if the one
who's been asking
about me

        is him.

Because why
would he ask
for my number
on behalf of
someone else?

The thought leaves
my belly buzzing,
blossoming with hope
as I respond with a half-truth:
I'll be back soon.

Rest Is Healing

And at the end of the week,
when I'm finally feeling
more like my old self,
Mami gives me the okay
to go back to work
        with accommodations.

I grumble as she lists
what my manager agreed to:
a stool to sit on,
more frequent breaks,
shorter hours.

I guess I should count myself
lucky to be working at all.

Farmacia Navarro

Waits for me like roses wait for rain, and
my first day back after my hiatus is a celebration.

Rosita passes pastelitos and Martica pours cafecitos.
My manager Santiago smiles wide, says,
Good to see you again. You'll be on register 3.
Doesn't mention my flare-up at all.

And I'm grateful.

Register 3 is the only one with a stool, but
as I settle in for my shift, I realize
no one notices, no one wonders why—
not Caleb or Suzi or Mauro.

And I breathe in relief.

Josue hovers around my register.
Between customers, he smiles shyly
and says, *I'm glad you're back.*

Doña Adelita Flutters In

Like the hummingbird that she is.
She greets me brightly and loudly,

There's my beautiful girl.

Everyone's gaze shifts to me,
but for once I don't mind
their attention on me.

I've missed you, cariño,
and Josue here looked as lost
as a Chihuahua without its bark.

I press my lips together
to hide the smile threatening to blossom
as Josue's cheeks flush all shades of pink.
But then Doña Adelita asks,

What kept you from us
for so long?

I falter,
my brain warring between
telling them   and not.

Catalina would say,
What's the big deal, anyway?
Santiago already knows, and
Doña Adelita would understand—
I know this like I know the beating
of my own heart.

Still, I can't help the small whisper
unfurling in my mind:
Would Josue understand?

Because worse than scaring away friends
is scaring away the boy you're beginning to like

who just might like you, too.

Catalina Would Tell Me

I'm too cautious,
    too scared
to take risks,
    too scared
to fail at everything.

And it's true.
I've never been good
at living
the way Catalina did—
large
and fearless
and free.

Maybe it's time to
stop being scared,
maybe it's time to
start living
like Doña Adelita said:
wildly, fully, unabashedly
    just the way I am.

So I Sow My Own Seeds of Truth

From Catalina to my illness to the restrictions

I sometimes have, and like a girasol

after a drought, I feel myself opening

wide and bright.

Josue

Doesn't turn away,
doesn't scatter pity over me,
doesn't even flinch
as understanding blossoms
on his face.

He says,
I remember the news
about your sister. We went to
middle school together.
I'm sorry.

He says,
I'm glad you're feeling better.
I missed you.
Hope unfurls
in my chest,
for new beginnings
in this Farmacia Navarro.

Doña Adelita seems to agree,
the way her eyes twinkle as she sings
"Somos novios"—an old Spanish love song—
all the way down the aisles.

And I Wonder

If maybe Doña Adelita is right—
I can learn to find beauty in the ashes,
to choose joy in the hard places,
to make art from broken pieces.

Maybe I'm a kaleidoscope after all,
brilliant   beautiful   brave,
reflecting a rainbow from my pain.

Maybe this is me

        bursting from the weeds

                beneath that rainbow

                        as I keep my promise

to my sister   and myself
imperfectly   but true.

The First, and the Last, and All the In-Betweens

BY JASMINE WARGA

We are driving
just like we did
that very first day
that wasn't technically your first day
or my first day
on Earth
but was the first day
of us,
which now feels like the only first
that matters.

Back then,
I was five
and you were
five months,
and we were new
to each other.

Today, I am seventeen
and you are thirteen
and two months
and four days
and I've done the math
because I want to count
every single
second,
every single
moment
that we have left.

Back then,
I sat in the back seat
and you were supposed to sit
next to me
but in a crate.
That didn't last long
because when Mom started the car,
you nudged your nose
against my hand,
and I opened the crate,
letting you out,
letting you in.

On that first drive
you curled up in my lap
and you stayed that way
the whole way home.

Today,
we are in the back seat
again
but you are not in a crate,
you are in my arms,
resting,
very still.

These days,
you don't have the energy
to jump anymore,
but do you remember
when I was ten
and you were so excited
to see me when I got home
from summer camp
that you jumped
and knocked me over?

And we fell to the floor
in a pile of giggles,
your tongue licking my face,
and me pretending like
that was gross
but really loving every second.

I have loved
every second.

I am thinking about that
as I stroke your head,
as I watch the trees blur,
as the car passes them.

The leaves are starting
to change from green
to yellow
and I know that soon they will be orange,
and soon you will not be here
to see them.

I stroke your soft fur
and try not to show you
my broken heart
though I know you know it
because you always know
everything.

Mom is driving
just like the day
that I brought you home.

Do you know that
dog was my first word?

Do you know that Mom
never planned to let me get a dog?
"No dogs, Nasrin," she said.
"Dogs, Mama, please," I said.

In Jordan, she did not grow up with dogs,
she did not understand why
I wanted to bring an animal
into our house,
but I begged
and begged
and begged,
and finally,
she agreed to go meet you,
and then we took you home
because it would've been impossible
not to because the moment
I met you
it was clear
so clear to even Mom
that we belonged
together.

Mom is wearing her sunglasses,
but I know her eyes are teary.
She keeps muttering your name
under her breath,
and it sounds like a wish,
like a prayer.

"Bounce, Bounce, Bounce," she says.
And yes, I named you Bounce.
Because when I was little
bounce was my favorite word.
It sounded magical.

You are magical.

I keep muttering
"I love you,"
but those three words
don't say what I want them to say.

They don't say
that you have been there
for every step,
every first day
since first grade,
my picture on the front stoop
you beside me,
your head in my lap
your head against my hip,
my arms around your neck,
your face pressed to my face,
the two of us,
thetwoofus,
no space.

The space is coming, though,
I know.

Every inch that the car moves
reminds me that we are getting closer,
and I don't think I'm ready,
but I know I have to be ready
because that's what you need,
and up until now,
you've always done what
I needed,
somehow always knowing,
somehow always anticipating.

Like in seventh grade,
when Tommy H.
broke my heart
when he announced
that he didn't find me pretty
and told everyone that I had
a mustache
and I came home crying so hard
I thought I would never catch my breath
and you came up right beside me
and curled your body next to me
and just waited it out,
your breathing
calming mine.

And after a while
I didn't feel so unlovable anymore
because you were there
lightly thumping your tail
gently nudging my hand
with your wet nose
and I felt like
Tommy H. had to be wrong
because there was no way
you could be wrong.

And then there was just last year,
when I came home from school
completely convinced I'd flunked my bio exam.
I could already see that red *F* emblazoned on the front,
and it felt like I was wearing it across my heart.

But when I flopped on the couch,
you flopped with me,
and I knew you didn't care about bio
or college admissions;

you only cared about snuggles
and kisses
and—

Oh—
Mom is pulling us into the parking lot
of the vet now
and this is where we came when we first got you
to make sure we had the right shots
and this is where we came the year
that you snuck up on the counter
and ate all the Eid treats
in one swoop
and this is where we came last week
when we found out that the growth
by your knee
was cancer
and that it wasn't going to get any better.

Mom tells me it's time,
but it can't be time
because that means it's time
to let you go
and I'm not ready.

Do you remember that one day
at the park?
When I let you off the leash
and we both ran as fast as we could
because I was trying to outrun the stress
of the PSAT
and all those vocab words that I had
shoved into my brain
hoping that they wouldn't slip out
but they kept slipping out,

so we went to the park to
try to forget about the words
and the logic problems
and you were running to run
and eventually I collapsed in the grass
and then you stopped running
even though I know you could have gone farther
but you stopped
to lie next to me.

It's time.

I help you get inside
and I don't really want to talk
about what happens next,
but I know that would be okay with you
because ours has always been a wordless love story
anyway
because sometimes the best love stories
are that way—
they aren't made by saying I love you;
they are forged by early-morning snuggles
and late-night lamplit walks
and too many nose kisses to name
and food snuck under the table
and dancing around my bedroom
and laughing—
until you,
I never knew that dogs could laugh.

I held you,
and you looked at me the whole time,
and even though I wanted to look away
because I was scared,
I kept looking into your big brown eyes

because you have always made me
brave.

I held you
and I felt you leave,
one moment,
exhales and inhales,
the next moment,
silence.

I kept holding you,
thinking maybe if I squeezed
hard enough,
you would come back.

But you didn't.

But now I'm walking out of this place
that I once brought you to
and every other time
you have walked out
with me.

Not today.
Today I only have your collar,
frayed and pink,
empty.

A leaf floats down from the sky.
I look at it—
it is green,
rimmed golden at the edges.

Do you remember
that afternoon
not too long ago

when we jumped in Mrs. Brook's
neatly crafted leaf piles
even though we were both too old
to do something so silly?

You were never too old.
You made me feel like I was
never too old.

I hold the leaf
and realize that I am walking out of here
without you,
but also always,
forever,
with you.

About the Authors

Alexandra Alessandri (she/her) is the author of several books for children, including *Isabel and Her Colores Go to School, The Enchanted Life of Valentina Mejía, Our World: Colombia, Lupita's Hurricane Palomitas*, and *Grow Up, Luchy Zapata*, which was a Junior Library Guild Gold Standard Selection. Her books have received numerous distinctions, including the Florida Book Award, the International Latino Book Award, the Américas Award Commended Title, and the International Literacy Association's 2022 Children's and Young Adults' Book Award in Primary Fiction. The daughter of Colombian immigrants, she is also an educator and a poet. Alexandra lives in Florida with her husband and son.

David Bowles (he/him) is a Mexican American author and translator from South Texas, where he works as an associate professor at the University of Texas Río Grande Valley. Among his award-winning books are *They Call Me Güero, The Prince & the Coyote*, and the graphic novel series Tales of the Feathered Serpent. With Guadalupe García McCall, he is also the coauthor of *Secret of the Moon Conch* and *Hearts of Fire and Snow*. David presently serves as the president of the Texas Institute of Letters.

Melanie Crowder (she/her) is an educator, speaker, and the acclaimed author of four YA novels, five middle grade novels, and two picture books. Her verse novel *Audacity* was a National Jewish Book Award Finalist and Jefferson Cup winner. Her historical YA novel *An Uninterrupted View of the Sky* was a Walden Award Finalist and Junior Library Guild Selection. A West Coast girl at heart, Melanie lives with her family under the big blue Colorado sky. She holds an MFA in writing and teaches at Vermont College of Fine Arts. For more information, visit her online at MelanieCrowder.com.

Margarita Engle (she/her) is the Cuban American author of books such as *Enchanted Air, Drum Dream Girl, Dancing Hands*, and *The Surrender Tree*, which received a Newbery Honor. She served as the 2017–2019 national Young People's Poet Laureate. Other awards include Pura Belpré Medals, the Golden Kite Award, Walter Honors, Américas Awards, the Jane Addams Children's Book Award, the PEN Literary Award, and the NSK Neustadt Prize. Recent young adult verse novels include *Wings in the Wild* and *Wild Dreamers*. Recent picture books include *Water Day* and *The Sculptors of Light*. Engle's next verse novel is *Island Creatures*, and her next picture book is *Eloísa's Musical Window*.

Eric Gansworth (he/him), S·ha-weñ na-sae' (Onondaga, Eel Clan), is a writer and artist from Tuscarora Nation. Author of thirteen books, his artwork has been exhibited widely. He's the Lowery Writer-in-Residence at Canisius University and has been a visiting professor at Colgate University. His work has received a Printz Honor, was long-listed for a National Book Award, and won an American Indian Library Association Youth Literature Award, a PEN Oakland Award, and an American Book Award. *Apple (Skin to the Core)* appeared on *TIME*'s Ten Best YA and Children's Books and on Chautauqua Institution's CLSC booklist. Gansworth's work has been supported by the Library of Congress, the New York Foundation for the Arts, the National Endowment for the Humanities, and the Lannan Foundation.

Robin Gow (it/fae/he and él y elle) is a poet, educator, and witch from rural Pennsylvania. It is the author of several poetry, middle grade, and young adult books, including the Lambda Literary Award-nominated *Dear Mothman*. It works as a community educator on topics of LGBTQIA2S+ and disability justice.

Mariama J. Lockington (she/her) is an adoptee, author, and educator. She has been telling stories and making her own books since the second grade, when she wore shortalls and flower leggings every day to school. Mariama's middle grade debut, *For Black Girls Like Me*, earned five starred reviews and was a *TODAY* Best Kids' Book of 2019. Her sophomore middle grade book, *In the Key of Us*, is a Stonewall Honor Book and was featured in *The New York Times*. Her debut young adult novel, *Forever Is Now*, was the 2024 winner of the Schneider Family Book Award. Mariama holds a master's in education from Lesley University and an MFA in poetry from San Francisco State University. She calls many places home but currently lives in Kentucky with her wife and an abundance of plants. When Mariama is not writing, she works as the director of the Professional Learning Series at the University of Kentucky's College of Education. You can find her on X @MariLock and on Instagram and TikTok @ForBlackGirlsLikeMe.

Laura Ruby (she/her) is a two-time National Book Award Finalist and the author of nearly a dozen novels, including *Thirteen Doorways, Wolves Behind Them All*, and the Printz Award-winning *Bone Gap*. Her poetry has appeared in such literary magazines as *Cleaver, Sugar House Review, Diode, Fantasy Magazine*, the *Clackamas Literary Review*, and *Nimrod*. She teaches fiction writing in the MFA programs of Hamline University and Queens University.

Padma Venkatraman (she/her) is the author of *Safe Harbor, The Bridge Home, Born Behind Bars, A Time to Dance, Island's End*, and *Climbing the Stairs*. Her books have sold over a quarter million copies, received over twenty starred reviews, and won numerous awards, including the Walter Dean Myers Award, South Asia Book Award, Golden Kite Award, and ALA Notable Book Selection. Her poetry has been published in *Poetry* magazine and nominated for a Pushcart Prize. An oceanographer by training, Padma loves teaching and sharing her love for reading and writing with others. You can learn more about her at PadmaVenkatraman.com or arrange a school visit via TheAuthorVillage.com/presenters/Padma-Venkatraman.

Jasmine Warga (she/her) is the #1 *New York Times* bestselling author of *A Rover's Story, The Shape of Thunder,* and *Other Words for Home*. Her books have won numerous awards, including a Newbery Honor. Her latest middle grade novel is *A Strange Thing Happened in Cherry Hall.* She currently lives in the Chicago area with her family.

Charles Waters (he/him) is a children's poet, author, anthologist, and actor. With Irene Latham he's cocreated *African Town*, winner of the Scott O'Dell Award for Historical Fiction; *Can I Touch Your Hair? Poems of Race, Mistakes, and Friendship*, which was named an NCTE Charlotte Huck Honor; and the anthology *The Mistakes That Made Us: Confessions from Twenty Poets*, a Junior Library Guild Selection. His book *Mascot* (cowritten with Traci Sorell) has won multiple awards, including a Jane Addams Children's Book Honor and an American Indian Youth Literature Honor. Find him online at CharlesWatersPoetry.com.

Kip Wilson (she/her) is the critically acclaimed YA author of the verse novels *White Rose, The Most Dazzling Girl in Berlin*, and *One Last Shot*. Awards for her books include the Malka Penn Award and the Julia Ward Howe Award, and her books have been named a Massachusetts Book Honor title, an Amelia Elizabeth Walden Award Finalist, and a *Los Angeles Times* Book Prize Finalist. Kip holds a PhD in German literature and is an enthusiastic high school library worker. Find her online at KipWilsonWrites.com and on Instagram @KipWilsonWrites.

Acknowledgments

Working on this collection of short stories in verse has been a dream come true, leaving me with many people to thank.

First off, a huge thanks to my agent, Roseanne Wells, for encouraging me to run with the idea and for being there every step of the way.

A likewise huge thanks to everyone on the Nancy Paulsen team at Penguin. Thank you to our editor, Stacey Barney, for believing in the merit of such an anthology and for the hard work on it from start to finish, and thank you to Jenny Ly and Sarah Sather for all the extra assistance as we wrapped things up. Thank you to Cindy De la Cruz for the beautiful and intricate care you took with the interior design. Thank you to Kaitlin Yang for the absolutely gorgeous cover design. Thanks to the production team of Brian Luster, Cindy Howle, Jacqueline Hornberger, and Aaron Burkholder for the indispensable attention to detail, and to the publicity and marketing teams for getting this book out into the world.

Finally, another huge thanks to each of the authors for writing such incredible stories and entrusting them to us: Alexandra Alessandri, David Bowles, Melanie Crowder, Margarita Engle, Eric Gansworth, Robin Gow, Mariama J. Lockington, Laura Ruby, Padma Venkatraman, Jasmine Warga, and Charles Waters. It has been such a pleasure working with each and every one of you. I absolutely love your wonderful words.

From all of us, an additional thanks to the supportive families, friends, and colleagues who have helped us along the way. Thank you specifically to Dahlia Adler for being so generous with the "So You Want to Edit a YA Anthology" advice, and to the editors of so many other YA anthologies already out there whose work served as fabulous models.

Last of all, perhaps the hugest thanks to *you*, dear reader, for picking up this collection. We appreciate you more than we could say!